W9-BEV-454

Shiny Little Things

Frank Stangle

1123

Shiny Little Things
Copyright © 2021 Frank Stangle

Produced and printed by Stillwater River Publications.
All rights reserved. Written and produced in the
United States of America. This book may not be reproduced
or sold in any form without the expressed, written
permission of the author(s) and publisher.

Visit our website at
www.StillwaterPress.com
for more information.

First Stillwater River Publications Edition

ISBN: 978-1-955123-45-7

Library of Congress Control Number: 2021917185

1 2 3 4 5 6 7 8 9 10
Written by Frank Stangle
Published by Stillwater River Publications,
Pawtucket, RI, USA.

*The views and opinions expressed
in this book are solely those of the author(s)
and do not necessarily reflect the views
and opinions of the publisher.*

To the memory of my mom,
who taught me to read —
Elizabeth Sarah O'Connell Stangle

And my pops,
who inspired me to be the best person I could be —
WWII Veteran S/Sergeant Peter H. Stangle

CONTENTS

AUTHOR'S NOTE

This story takes place in the early 1980s. Kids didn't have cell phones, or have their faces buried in a screen twelve hours a day. They went outside and actually played games like tag, whiffle ball, and hide and seek. Kids were allowed to be kids. Groups of them sometimes sat in the beds of trucks while being taken to events such as baseball practice, football games, and picnics. They rolled around in the backs of station wagons, without seatbelts or airbags, and were allowed to be let loose at amusement parks to enjoy time with their friends. It was the best time of life; to just have fun, without any thought of worry. A kid couldn't wait to take a ride on their new bike to show it off to their best buds and see what kind of adventure they could get into.

The kids in this story got to enjoy that simpler time; they played, and had fun, but one day, in an instant, things changed for them. Their lives and everything around them were turned upside down. They spent the rest of the day trying to make things right, and in the process they learned something about themselves and the difference they could make in the world.

In everyone's life, age betrays youth, and at that point we start to become adults. It happens differently for everyone, but it doesn't need to be a permanent condition. So refuse to grow up, because age is only in body and not in mind.

I hope you enjoy this story as much as I did writing it for you.

1

FALLING

"Nooooo! Noooo! Stop! Stooooooooop! Please don't!" screamed a young boy in his early teens. He was suspended over a large pond.

He dropped about twenty feet into the water and made a big splash. He popped his head out. He felt okay; nothing hurt, nothing seemed to be broken. He survived the fall. Since he was okay, he swam toward shore.

He heard a few more splashes. Something entered the water with him. *What's that?* he thought to himself. He knew that something was swimming in there with him. He felt it tug at his feet and clothes. The pressure on his legs pulled him under. He kicked, squirmed and tried to free himself to get away, but the more he struggled, the weaker he became.

He held his breath and tried to get to the surface, but he couldn't. His last attempt to make it out almost got him there. He wailed and flailed his arms and tried to grab for something that wasn't there. This allowed him to break free and gave him a chance to make it to the surface.

He needed a breath. He could feel the oxygen leave his body, that feeling you get when you hold your breath as long as you can. The feeling of suffocation and anxiety. Panic not just set in, but consuming his every thought. He was very scared. He couldn't breathe. He was underwater and tried anything to take a breath, to get air in his lungs one more time.

2

MR. MCGHEEZER

Two boys rode their bicycles down an old dirt path in a large field. The path was part of a farm owned by an old man named McGhee. The boys noticed on the other side of the path, over a barbed-wire fence, was a wooded area that had overtaken an old cemetery that dated back from the 1700s to the mid-1850s. The two saw that the cemetery was not like modern cemeteries. The tombstones were thinner, smaller and broken. Some seemed to be missing, as if they were made of wood that just rotted away. It was hard to tell exactly what was in there because of the overgrown trees, vines. and thicket.

The first boy's name was Randal "Rusty" Van Buren. He was a fifteen-year-old redhead with a crew cut. He was big for his age and had a stomach that resembled a beer belly, like a man who drank too much might have. He was big in stature, but not fat. He was well into maturing like a little man and even had chin whiskers. He was rather agile for his size because of years of playing peewee football, wrestling, and baseball. Rusty did not have a learning disability but was slow to grasp things that an average kid would pick up easily. It stemmed from attention deficit issues and his mind tended to wander a lot. This resulted in Rusty repeating the first grade.

Rusty had no filter when he spoke. He said what he said. It came out blunt, rash, and he never really meant anything to be harsh. He tried to be funny in his own way. He really held nothing back and because of his size, not too many people questioned the way he put things. He had one of the worst potty mouths for a kid of his age. It could make a sailor's mother cry.

Rusty commented, "Hey Skeeter, we probably need to go and explore that cemetery over there sometime soon. It looks kinda interesting, maybe we could set up the tents and spend the night, see if any specters show up—*boooo ohhhh ahhhhh*," as he made a creepy scary ghostly noise in Skeeter's face.

"Come on, let's get goin'," Skeeter replied as he pushed Rusty out of his personal space.

Skeeter was fourteen years old. His father nicknamed him this because as a toddler he was all over the place, like a mosquito. He got into trouble a lot. He played with stuff he shouldn't get into and climbed up where he didn't belong. His father thought he was a little pain in the behind and the name stuck. Skeeter was a little slower in the physical maturation department, and not as big as Rusty. He was a runt, about a foot shorter and half his friend's size, skinny and very small for his age. He was a late bloomer. Unlike Rusty, however, he was very intelligent and able to figure things out easily.

Skeeter had long dark hair and always needed it cut. The back hung far past his shoulders and he constantly shoved it out of his field of vision because his bangs were always in his eyes. Skeeter was rarely seen not wearing his favorite rock T-shirt of AC/DC. The kind with a white chest and black three-quarter-length sleeves.

The two boys were best friends since they met in first grade, around nine years ago, and despite the size difference, Skeeter was not afraid of sticking up for himself when Rusty decided to play rough. This had definitely toughened Skeeter up, making him able to handle himself in a difficult situation. The two were joined at the hip, inseparable you could say. When they were not together each were out of sorts.

The two boys stopped riding down the path and prepared to sneak through a barbed-wire fence that protected Mr. McGhee's backyard.

"What are you waiting for?" asked Rusty as he sat on the ground and pulled at his pants which he'd just ripped on the sharp barbed wire as he passed through.

"I don't think we should do this anymore," objected Skeeter. "Let's just go all the way around the front of his house. He always gets so mad when he catches us."

"Don't be such a sissy. We do this all the time. If we go all the way around, it'll take forever. I don't even see him anywhere."

"That's just it: we never see him, until he catches us. I'm gonna go around."

"Why are you being such a Nancy boy? It's gonna be okay. We can just run for it like every other time if he comes out. Come on. I'll hold the wire up for you to get through easier. It's getting dark and we are running out of daylight."

"Okay I guess, but next time we need to go around."

Skeeter succumbed to Rusty's peer pressure, handed the bikes over, and crawled under the bottom wire as Rusty held it up for him.

The two boys rode cautiously to try and avoid being spotted by Mr. McGhee.

"Hey, what are you two hoodlums doing there?!" shouted the old man. "This is my property and I don't want you cuttin' through here no more. I told you that before."

Mr. McGhee was an elderly man in his seventies. Years of

working the fields had kept him active and strong, but had taken its toll on his appearance. His hands were worn and beat up from the daily tasks on the farm, and his face and skin were tattered from years of exposure to the sun. His wife died a few years back and that had made him not the most pleasant man to be around. It had given him a bad reputation in town as being a crotchety old man.

He had slicked back white hair that was a bit long for a man of his age. His beard was scraggly and always needed a trim. He was tall—over six feet with a barrel chest—and during his time in the army they had replaced one of his missing lower front teeth with a gold one. You could tell he had enjoyed some of his own handcrafted brews throughout his life by the way his belly stuck out and the purple hue of his plump big nose. His voice was deep and commanded the attention of everyone who heard it. He would never be caught wearing anything other than his jean overalls and a white pocket tee unless he was going to church or a funeral, but this old man hadn't been to church in years.

"Oh, Jesus look!" yelled Skeeter. "What should we do?"

Being halfway through the yard, the boys were past the point of no return. Going back was not an option. They had made this trek many times over the summer without incident, but Skeeter's fears were warranted, for this time they were caught.

"Go! Go! Go! Let's go, all we have to do is get past his yard and that old dirty bastard can't do a thing about it!" yelled Rusty.

BOOM! BOOM! Mr. McGhee fired two shotgun blasts straight up into the air and startled the boys. It was only rock salt. McGhee had caught the boys before and had no intention of hurting them; he just wanted to give them another warning.

They rode as fast as they could across the back of Mr. McGhee's yard. It was about three hundred feet long and was the only part of the McGhee property that was well groomed. He did the upkeep on the grass in honor of his wife's memory. She had always maintained a very tidy yard and garden.

The boys pedaled as fast as they could and rode to the other side of his fence line. Once they were there, they passed through the wire. It was a cumbersome task because they were scared and in a hurry, but they made it through. Skeeter hopped on his bike and started to ride away, but not Rusty. He stopped and stared up at Mr. McGhee standing on his porch. He knew they were far enough away from him that he couldn't do anything.

Rusty looked over at Skeeter and chuckled, "Stop, I got an idea."

Skeeter wanted to keep going, but came back to see what Rusty was up to.

Rusty reached down into his backpack, pulled out a Roman candle, lit it, and started to holler, "Take this Old Man McGheezer, you old dirty bastard!" Rusty called Mr. McGhee "Old Man McGheezer" behind his back to be funny, but this time it was about disrespect.

The fuse on the firework burned down and started to spit out colored fireballs. Rusty pointed it at Mr. McGhee's house and shot it straight at him. The boys were far enough away that the Roman candle couldn't have hit him even if Rusty wanted it to.

"Stop that!" cried Skeeter. He grabbed at Rusty's arm.

"No, this is way too much fun."

"You're gonna hurt yourself. Come on. Let's stick to the plan," Skeeter tried to convince Rusty to stop and move on.

Mr. McGhee barked, "Get outta here, you two little good-for-nothings!"

Rusty lit another Roman candle to irritate Mr. McGhee after the first one burned out.

Mr. McGhee started to walk down the steps of the back porch as if he was going to chase the two.

"Oh no! Let's go!" cried Skeeter. "He's coming after us."

"He's never gonna catch me!" screamed Rusty, and he threw the Roman candle towards the house.

Mr. McGhee stood in his yard, laughed, and thought to himself, *Ha ha, I could never catch those two little whippersnappers*. He went down and made sure the Roman candle that Rusty threw was fully extinguished.

Rusty and Skeeter left the area fast. The path was rough, rocky and hard to manage while on bikes. They rode until they were too tired to continue, hopped off, and pushed the bikes for a while. They started to tell stories about Mr. McGhee.

"I heard these guys talking in town," commented Rusty. "They said that Mr. McGhee was a serial murderer. He killed his wife and spent forty years in jail, and that's the reason why his backyard is so nice is because he has his wife buried there."

"That's not true at all. My parents said that he was some kind of war hero back in World War II. He had something to do with shooting down German planes. Eventually he got shot himself, or hurt somehow, and received the Purple Heart in the Battle of the Bulge," mentioned Skeeter. "Right before they grounded me for soaping his truck windows, they said he was mayor of Roaring Springs about thirty years ago. He was well respected and they couldn't believe how mean he got when his wife died. The people in town started rumors about him. He made some enemies when he became so standoffish. This happens everywhere, especially in small towns where there are a lot of nosy people and everyone is in everybody else's business."

"Well I'm not sure about all that hero stuff," sniveled Rusty. "All I know is that crazy old douche nozzle would have killed us if he caught us. I don't think I ever want to see him again."

The boys told stories of all the shenanigans they pulled on Mr. McGhee.

"Yeah, that was great. We soaked the bars of soap in warm water and they became really soft. When we smeared them all over windows of his truck, it was so thick I bet it took him a week to clean it off, and the marks from the eggs we threw last Halloween are still on the side of his house," laughed Rusty.

"I'm not thinking it was so funny now, Rust. My parents grounded me for a week. I thought my dad was gonna lock me up for a whole year when he found out what I did."

"What about when we did Ding Dong Ditch? You rang the bell. He came out the second time and chased us. I thought I was gonna get caught. He almost got me. He's fast for an old man."

"He's not really fast. You're just, big, fat, and slow. It was kinda really funny tho', watchin' you run around tryin' to get away from an old man like that."

The boys laughed, rolled around on the ground, and had a big belly laugh together. Once they had enough of a break, they got back on their bikes and continued to tell stories about Mr. McGhee as they rode down the rocky path.

3

FIREFIGHT

The boys finally reached their original destination. It was a stream about twenty feet wide that ran for miles and miles.

"You know what Rusty?" asked Skeeter.

"Huh?"

"This is my most favorite place in the world to be. Someday I want to travel north and see if we can find where the stream starts."

"Yeah, I like it here too. It's calm and seems cooler in the summer. The sun doesn't beat down all day 'cause of the shade trees."

"Travelin' north can be an adventure for us another day."

The stream had an old, broken-down wooden bridge that allowed horses and carriages to pass over it a long time ago, but it was unsafe to walk on. The only thing that remained was one wooden beam that was still in place. If you were careful and balanced yourself very well you could make it across. If you did happen to fall, most likely you wouldn't get hurt. It was only about a four-foot drop and the water was not deep. It was a lazy stream and did not move very fast.

Fishing would not be great because no one stocked it. When it rained hard, at certain times of the year, the water level would rise and flood the outlying areas.

Where the boys played was surrounded by a large wooded area, much like a forest. It was a dense spot; not too many people knew about it. Since the highway went through on the other side of town decades ago, this area had long been forgotten. The flooding made this property undesirable for development, and since it was far out of the way, it was as if the boys had the whole world to themselves. It was their own little private paradise.

One hundred yards or so from the decrepit old bridge were the remains of an old stone farmhouse the forest had reclaimed. Any signs of lumber that was part of the original building had long been taken by insects and Mother Nature. The boys talked about one day rebuilding it for the most awesome fort ever.

The stone structure that remained of the house was not fun for the boys to play in, but there was an old hole in the side of a hill not far from the stone foundation that was perfect. It was a root cellar that used to be where the owners of the house would store crops for the winter. The boys called this "The Cave." The door had long been rotted away, but stones remained that made an archway for the entrance. The supports inside were still intact. It seemed safe for the boys to spend time in. They had built a tunnel leading into the entrance using a lot of debris and brush. Anyone who stumbled upon this area would never know it was there.

Next to the large foundation there was also a smaller one. This was known as a summer kitchen. Older farmhouses had a separate smaller building away from the main house that was used for cooking. It kept the main house from getting too hot in the summer months. The boys always thought that the summer kitchen would be a better place to make their fort. It was smaller and more manageable for their carpentry skills.

The two boys were not here to play in the Cave or around the house though. They had more important things to do. Over the last few weeks, they had built two war bunkers. One on each side of the stream. Rusty's bunker was basically made of branches and limb wood from broken trees, placed haphazardly in a mound. It was not much of a structure, just a bunch of sticks and branches set in a semicircle that faced towards Skeeter's bunker.

Skeeter's bunker, however, was constructed much better. He elevated his about five feet off the ground. He put time and effort into its construction. He used tools, like a hammer, saw, nails, and binding twine that he brought from his dad's workshop. He had time over the past weekend to work on "The Fortress," as he called it, while Rusty was away with his mother. It was always just the two of them; Rusty's dad wasn't home a lot as he was in the army. Every other weekend Rusty and his mother took a trip to see his grandma in a different state.

Skeeter built his bunker to have a slight aerial advantage over Rusty's. It didn't look safe. It could never hold Rusty's weight, but since Skeeter was a lot smaller, it would perform well for what the boys had planned.

It was summertime and around nine o'clock in the evening, and although the sun had set, the sky still had enough twilight to allow the boys to see. They were on summer break from school and didn't have a curfew. Each had told their respective mothers they were staying at the other boy's home, so they wouldn't worry or know what the boys were up to. Their mothers wanted them home by dark, but for what they had planned, the dark was the best time to do it.

Rusty inquired of Skeeter, "You know the rules, right?" as he shook a can of starting fluid.

"Yeah, I got it. We're going to fill these garbage bags up with starting fluid and as the gas fills the bag up like a balloon, we'll tie them in the trees just above our bunkers. Then we'll shoot bottle rockets and try to blow each other's up. The first one that explodes the other guy's bag wins. Kaboom!"

"You got it punk," mocked Rusty. Both boys laughed, smacked hands, and separated.

Skeeter ran over the bridge and crossed the creek to his side. He prepared his bag at the Fortress. Rusty did the same at his pile of sticks. The boys filled the bags with starting fluid.

"Hey Skeeter, mine is not filling up. It's just staying floppy like a wet paper bag!" hollered Rusty from across the stream.

"Don't worry, just spray the whole can in there, tie it off, and hang it in the tree. I'm sure that it'll go off when I hit it."

Rusty looked at it and shook his head in disbelief. "This is never gonna work."

"Yes it will. Trust me. It's gonna be a blast."

It was dark and a three-quarter waning moon lit the sky just enough to see. Each boy had a backpack full of various fireworks, mostly bottle rockets and Roman candles. Once each was ready to begin the battle, the plan was to signal with a single bottle rocket shot into the air.

"You can stop now and go home, if you want. I won't think you're scared," jeered Skeeter. "Look at that pathetic attempt at a fort. It'll never protect you."

Rusty snarled back, "I'm gonna make you look like a little girl. When this is all over, you're gonna go run home and cry to your mommy."

"There won't be anything left of you for your mom to bury when I'm through with you."

"I hope you brought a bigger army than what you have now if you think you're gonna do something like that."

With that, each boy sent up a flare to signal to the other that they were ready and the firework war began.

Skeeter brought a lot of matches that he had saved. He got off the first shot. Skeeter had a secret weapon. He brought a piece of pipe an inch and a half in diameter to use as a makeshift bazooka launcher. He lit a bottle rocket, put it in the end of the tube, and pointed it at Rusty's garbage bag.

Skeeter thundered, "Bring death and hellfire from above!" and shot a downward trajectory bottle rocket to Rusty's bag just behind his bunker. The boys fired bottle rockets back and forth for a couple minutes. They were close to each other's bag but neither had hit their mark. Neither had that perfect shot.

What Skeeter didn't know was that Rusty had his own secret weapon. Rusty pulled out a pack of cigarettes that he had stolen from his mom. It wasn't a full pack, but enough to give him a rapid-fire advantage.

The advantage that Rusty had was he didn't need to light a new match for each bottle rocket like Skeeter did. Once Rusty had a cigarette lit, he could line up as many bottle rockets as fast as he could manage and light each one of them with the hot end of the cigarette. This could allow Rusty to send ten bottle rockets to Skeeter's one.

Rusty screamed over to Skeeter, "I got you now you smelly little turd bag!" and he lit up a cigarette. He didn't smoke. Consequently, he gagged as he inhaled the little tar stick, the smoke causing him to cough and choke. It hindered his ability to attack. While Rusty was incapacitated, Skeeter continued his onslaught. Once Rusty had his composure back, he set a bunch of bottle rockets off at Skeeter rapid-fire. One at a time they flew toward Skeeter's Fortress from his launching platform atop his pile of twigs. The launching platform was just a one-by-eight piece of wood placed at a slight incline, pointing toward Skeeter's Fortress.

The boys continued to shoot back and forth at each other. The distance between the two forts was so great that neither's aim was on target and each boy's bag was still unburnt. Rusty had shot a lot of rockets off, but Skeeter had the advantage. He was more accurate.

Skeeter loaded his launcher another time, pointed, and aimed. The bottle rocket flew out, grazed Rusty's plastic garbage bag, and bounced off into the woods. After about fifty tries that was the closest that Skeeter had gotten.

Despite the fact that neither boy had gotten a kill shot, both had so much fun that they lost track of time. It was late and neither boy had any intention of stopping until a garbage bag of starting fluid had erupted into flames and one was declared the winner.

The battle raged on. Both boys continued to load and shoot pyrotechnics of various sizes towards each other.

Rusty shot a single bottle rocket that skipped off the front of Skeeter's bunker and startled him. He jumped and dropped a lit bottle rocket from the back of his launcher and it landed in his backpack, filled with his remaining fireworks. It proceeded to flare up while in the backpack. This caused the other fireworks to be lit sequentially inside his pack. Skeeter looked down. He was elevated off the ground about four feet and was suspended over the creek bank. He wanted to jump, but his senses were askew because of the dark. He wasn't sure of the right thing to do. He needed to decide whether to jump or try to put the fire out. That was when the backpack erupted in a fiery explosion.

On the other side of the stream, Rusty knew he got off a good shot; not a coup de grâce, but one that made Skeeter back up and pay attention. Rusty laughed until he saw Skeeter jump around, and then the explosion.

Rusty, fearing for Skeeter's safety, jumped up from his protected position in the bunker and raced straight through the water. He got to the fort soaking wet and didn't see Skeeter at all. The fireworks from Skeeter's bag were still going off. This did not trouble Rusty because he was more concerned whether Skeeter was okay.

Rusty looked in Skeeter's fort first and didn't see him. This worried Rusty. Then from the corner of his eye, he saw movement in the water. It was Skeeter, fifteen feet upstream. He ran over to his sidekick to make sure he was all right.

"Get up, get up, wake up!" begged Rusty with deep concern. Skeeter was still and facedown, in the mud. It was dark, but by this time the moon was directly overhead and allowed the boys to see well. Not only was the night lit up by the moon, but Skeeter's bunker was engulfed in flames and lit the surrounding area. Rusty grabbed Skeeter and shook him.

Rusty cried out again with great concern, "Come on buddy, get up! You okay?"

Rusty saw that Skeeter regained consciousness in his arms, grinned and remarked, "Wow, I was worried about you, I thought you were dead, deader than a doorknocker, I thought I killed you," and he gave Skeeter big hug.

The phrase is deader than a doornail, but Rusty had a habit of saying proverbs incorrectly.

Skeeter looked up at Rusty and in a dazed voice responded, "You might be big, you fat tub 'a lard, but you ain't big enough to kill me. I'm okay, now let me go." He squirmed to get out of Rusty's grasp.

Rusty looked at Skeeter's fort and sneered. "Look at the Fortress! It's on fire! That was a perfect bullseye."

"Aaahhh, no, you got lucky, there is no way you pulled that shot off on purpose," ridiculed Skeeter. "I dropped a bottle rocket into my bag and it ignited the rest."

"No excuses Skeet, you know I did that. I won. Your fort is a pile of ash," jeered Rusty in triumph. "I am the winner!"

"You are a wiener all right, but it's not true that you won the war," retorted Skeeter. The blood boiled inside his little body. This happens to some people when they are called a liar and they are not one, or when they lose a game and couldn't stand to be beaten. He felt the anger grow inside and fumed. "It was a lucky shot and I won't say you won," and he pushed Rusty away.

Skeeter didn't have enough mass to move Rusty at all, but in retaliation, Rusty pushed Skeeter back and shoved him down.

Skeeter fell and found himself back in the water again. He heard Rusty taunt, "Skill or lucky shot your fort is burned to a crisp, so I will take that as a win." Rusty offered Skeeter his hand to pull him up out of the muck.

Skeeter was upset. He refused Rusty's gesture and tried to get up by himself. Skeeter pushed off a rock that was in the water to give himself leverage. He looked down and noticed something shimmering, reflecting the fire that burned up what was left of his fort. The object was buried in the muck, only a small portion visible. It looked like a shiny cue ball, some kind of glass orb. Skeeter grabbed at it and plucked it out of the mud.

The two boys looked up at Skeeter's bunker and noticed that the bag of starting fluid had ignited and set the surrounding trees on fire. Skeeter put the object in his pocket and the boys worked together to extinguish the fire. They grabbed what they could of what was left of the Fortress and pulled the burning wood into the creek. This slowed the fire down, and with a little effort, the remaining fire was doused with water. They didn't want to have a forest fire on their hands.

"Wow! That could've really got out of control quickly, but since your bag is now burned, I will officially declare myself the winner of this war and wish you luck with the next one loser. We better go now," proclaimed Rusty as the boys stomped out the hot embers of what was once Skeeter's Fortress.

"I spent a whole week on the Fortress and now it's gone. I thought we could've used it more than once," snapped Skeeter, "but I will not admit defeat." Skeeter looked with disgust at the pile of burned wood that remained of his bunker.

It was late and the boys gathered up their stuff for the ride home.

Skeeter almost forgot about the orb. He reached into his pocket and asked, "What about this thing? Rust, what is it?"

The moonlight shone on the orb, but not enough to make out any detail. Skeeter dunked it in the water to wash it off.

Rusty remarked, "Let's go get my lighter."

They took a hike over the old bridge to Rusty's bunker with the orb. It was a perfectly round glasslike sphere, about the size of a baseball. Glasslike was a true description because it resembled glass. What the kids didn't realize was that it might have felt like a glass ball, but it wasn't. It was a force field that held everything inside it together in a small, tight, round, package. The boys could hold it, and never realize what it truly was.

Rusty lit his lighter and the boys began to examine the orb a bit better. It was still dark and the lighter did not cast sufficient light for a proper look. They looked at it under the flickering flame. The boys noticed that there were two figurines inside the orb, almost as if they were suspended in water.

Skeeter looked at the two images inside the globe and, watching them as the lighter burned, stated, "Look close Rusty. They're moving in there. They look like they're alive. I know what that one is: a cherub. My mom makes them. You know, she has them all over my yard. Those two things seem to be fighting."

"Hey, you're right Skeet. They are moving. That's creepy," replied Rusty. "See that other thing, it looks like a dragon. What is this thing and how long has it been in the creek bed?"

"OUCH!" shouted Rusty as he burned his finger on the hot lighter and dropped it into the water.

"Great job jerk bag," snapped Skeeter in an angry tone. "Now what are we gonna do?"

Rusty reached into the water, grabbed the lighter, and tried to get it to work, but it wouldn't. He said, "This thing is as useful as boobs on a nun," before tossing it into the thicket.

"Hey, don't you have a flashlight in your pack?" inquired Skeeter.

"Yeah, you're right," answered Rusty. "Stay here, I'll be right back."

Rusty made his way over to his backpack and dug out his flashlight. He brought it to Skeeter. The two boys shined the light deep into the orb and examined it.

"That's so much better. Look at this thing," said Rusty. "I can see it so much clearer than with just the itty-bitty lighter flame."

"It's mesmerizing Rusty. I can't take my eyes off of it. It looks like an optical illusion. Those things in there look so lifelike but it can't be real." Skeeter stared into the orb as if he was in a trance.

"This thing must have been in the creek for years. Look Skeeter, they're fightin' in there."

"I know. I'm watchin'. It looks like they're wrestling."

"Have they been doin' this the whole time that they were in the water?"

"I don't know, Rusty. We just found it. I guess so; it doesn't look like they have a referee, scoreboard, or a time limit," Skeeter said sarcastically.

The boys looked on as if they were in a high school gym and the two creatures were having a wrestling bout. This was all too familiar to the boys, for both were members of the high school wrestling team.

"Is that thing a dragon? It doesn't really look like a dragon."

"It's not, it's a gargoyle."

"What's a gargoyle?"

"Gargoyles are those dragon-like statues with wings that sit up on top of buildings. They're supposed to scare away evil spirits or something like that."

"Well the gargoyle is winning. Look! Look! Look! The gargoyle has the cherub on his back! He's gonna get the pin. Aww nope the cherub got away; escape: one point.

"Rusty there's something written in there. It's floating on a banner. You know; the kind that flies behind a plane at the beach advertising for a local car dealership or some rock concert."

Rusty looked at what was written inside the orb and grumbled, "I don't understand what that is, it's a bunch of gibberish. It's probably some foreign language that you can't understand."

The inscription written in the globe was in Latin and read:

SIT EOS EXCITARE.

Skeeter used the flashlight to try and read the phrase. He said it aloud but he didn't know what it meant.

In a soft voice Skeeter murmured, "*Sitto eos excitement,*" but that was nowhere close to what was written in the orb.

Skeeter tried it again, "*Sit eoso excitare.*" but this was still not correct.

"That sounds like Spanish. Let me see that," huffed Rusty, and grabbed the orb from Skeeter's hand. "Boy I wish I paid more attention in Miss Roble's Spanish 101 class now. Let's go. I'm so hungry I could eat an ox." He looked at it, shrugged his shoulders, and tossed it back. Skeeter wasn't ready and almost dropped it.

"Hey be careful you big tool sack! It looks cool. I don't want to break it!" shouted Skeeter.

Skeeter looked at the orb and shouted the phrase in a forceful voice, one more time, ***"SIT EOS EXCITARE!"***

This time Skeeter nailed it and read the phrase correctly.

Something strange happened. The orb shook, rose from Skeeter's hand, and floated in midair, like some kind of dime-store magic trick. It hovered and spun with bluish sparks coming out of it like a glass plasma lamp or a Tesla coil.

There was a big crack of lightning that the orb called out of the sky. It blew the boys off their feet with such violent force that they landed several yards away. In the confusion the orb dropped to the ground and the boys lost track of it. They were not hurt but they were scared, startled, and could not hear because they were deafened by the loud clap of thunder.

4

RED RAINDROPS FALLING
ON OUR HEADS

Skeeter and Rusty survived the explosion. Both felt the effects of the percussion, the temporary hearing loss and ringing in the ears that was associated with a blast of that magnitude. The two soon regained their composure, scrambled to their bikes, hopped on, and started to head home in a daze.

The lightning strike was not only unnatural but also very surrealistic, the way it came out of nowhere on such a calm, clear night.

They were not sure what they had done, but they knew what happened was freaky and wanted to get away from there to the safety of their homes.

The boys pedaled their bikes as fast as they could and avoided obstacles in their way. It was dark but they could see where they were going because the moon was, somehow, still out. The lightning bolt did something weird. It had started a rainstorm. They could feel and hear the ominous sound of the storm as it came up behind them.

They made it to Mr. McGhee's yard. They needed to stop at the barbed wire. This slowed them down drastically. They were never going to outrun the storm at this pace. They sensed the rain as it got closer. Rusty was first; he threw his bike over the fence and proceeded to climb through.

Skeeter was just behind. He was not as strong as Rusty and had problems getting his bike over the fence.

"Rusty stop, help me, I need to get my bike over. I need help!" screamed Skeeter.

Rusty had already ridden away from the area and needed to turn around after he heard Skeeter's cries for help. He came back and offered assistance.

"Hand it over, I'll grab it," commanded Rusty.

Stopping at the fence allowed the rain to catch up. Both boys started to get soaking wet. They passed through Mr. McGhee's yard and needed to do the same thing on the other side.

The boys continued to get wet, but they noticed something strange. They could still see where they were going. Skeeter looked up and noticed that the moon shined brightly to help guide them home. He thought to himself how weird that was, considering they were being rained on.

Skeeter locked up the brakes on his bike and slid to a stop in front of Rusty. "Rusty look up, the moon is out. So are the stars, too. That's very weird."

Rusty stared at the lit moon with a peculiar look on his face.

"Yeah Skeeter, that's really weird. The rain isn't falling out of the sky. It's coming from the ground, and look at your face. It's red and dirty. The rain is red! You look like you're covered in blood. This is really freaky. Let's get out of here!" exclaimed Rusty in a scared voice.

"So are you, I don't get it Rusty. I don't care what's going on. I just want to get the hell out of here and to my house. We can come back tomorrow and see what happened."

A deluge of red rainwater rose from the ground. As it went up it could not stay in the sky, and eventually gravity brought it back to down. It started out as a slow drizzle, but the longer the boys were in it the heavier it became. It was like some kind of odd golf course sprinkler system on steroids. They didn't understand what happened; all they knew was none of this was normal and they weren't sticking around to try and figure it out.

The boys pedaled as hard as they could. The two sped toward Skeeter's house as fast as their legs would take them. Rusty had been behind Skeeter ever since they passed through the second barbed wire fence. The red rain made the ground muddy and loose. Rusty was out of breath and started to tire. This caused him to slip off the trail, and he rode into a ravine, already filled with a few inches of water.

Skeeter noticed that Rusty was not behind him anymore and slowed down. Skeeter turned around and raced back to see if he could find him. The red rain seemed like an impenetrable wall of water and it stung Skeeter's face as he rode right past him. Rusty saw Skeeter as he tried to climb out of the ravine and called out his name.

"Skeeter, here I am!"

Rusty was not hurt. He just couldn't climb out of the ravine because of how muddy and steep it was. Skeeter looked down and saw Rusty in the ditch and teased, "Whatcha do that for?"

"I didn't plan to fall down here. It was an accident. Do something, get me outta here."

"I'll look for something to get you out; stay there and don't go anywhere."

"Where am I gonna go?! I'm stuck down here; just get something to help me out!"

Rusty was definitely in a panic at this point. He was trapped and just wanted to get out.

Skeeter ran to the edge of the field, to a tree line. He wasn't sure if he would even find something that *could* work to get Rusty out. He held his hair out of his vision and scanned the area. He had something in mind but nothing he saw looked useful. He searched for a few moments and found what he was looking for. It was a widow-maker from an old oak tree, or rather a former widow-maker; the freak storm had knocked the dead limb from the tree before it could live up to its name. Skeeter struggled to move the long, cumbersome branch to where Rusty was stuck.

The whole time, Rusty continued to claw and fight his way out of the ravine to no avail. Skeeter carried the branch to where Rusty was and leaned it into the ditch. It acted as a makeshift ladder that would assist Rusty out of the ravine. He started to climb out, but in his haste, he forgot all about his bike.

"Your bike, don't forget your bike!" exclaimed Skeeter.

Rusty let go of the branch and grabbed his bike, which now was covered with mud. The bottom of the ravine was really starting to fill up with runoff rainwater. This made it harder and more slippery to get out. Rusty grabbed the branch and climbed one more time. He stayed as surefooted as he could, considering the circumstances. Near the top of the bank, Skeeter clutched and pulled on his shirt. This assisted Rusty out of the deep ravine.

"That ditch was only five feet, but with all that rain and not being able to get any traction, it may as well have been the Grand Canyon," remarked Rusty in a weary and tired voice.

The boys, with a boost of adrenaline, rode their bikes home and got wetter and wetter. They arrived at Skeeter's driveway.

Skeeter shouted over the rain, "Your house is so far away! Just stay here for tonight. We told your mom that's what you were doing."

Rusty nodded yes. "Good idea. I don't wanna ride home in this anyway."

The boys raced up Skeeter's long driveway. Dropped their bikes at the porch steps and stripped down to their skivvies. Skeeter noticed something out of the corner of his eye before they ran into the house. Something moved, but it couldn't have, it must've been his imagination. The night's events had taken their toll on him and made him see things.

Skeeter's mom yelled to the boys, "Hey, you two better not be tracking all that water in my house! I just cleaned it!" as she lay on the couch, almost falling asleep.

"Okay Mom."

"We won't Mrs. Copeland."

Skeeter's mom heard the rain, but she had no idea what had happened to the boys.

They ran upstairs and saw each other better in the light.

"Look at you bro, you're a mess," Skeeter told Rusty as he stood there covered from head to toe in a blood-colored tint. "You go hop in the shower. I'll go get some of my brother's clothes from his room so you have something to wear. He won't miss them because he's at college."

The boys were both covered in what appeared to be blood. It couldn't be blood though. Neither boy was hurt, and there was too much of it.

Skeeter ran into his brother's room and grabbed the clothes while Rusty took a shower. When Rusty was done, Skeeter did the same and cleaned himself up.

Both sat in Skeeter's room at the window. They looked out and talked about what had happened.

"I can't believe what we just saw, is that even possible?" questioned Rusty.

"I know, right; what was that thing I found? It was some kind of crystal ball. It looked like a snow globe. Hey! Let's call it the Snow Globe," added Skeeter, "and what was up with those two things inside it? What were they doing? It looked like they were wrestling or something."

"How do you think the Snow Globe got there and what

are the chances that you would just find it? Those creatures were alive in there. The whole situation seems pretty freaky to me. Do you still have it?"

"No, I don't know what happened to it after the lightning strike. It's gotta still be there."

Skeeter talked on and on about what happened. He looked over and saw that Rusty had closed his eyes and fallen asleep. Skeeter wasn't that fortunate. He sat at the window and stared at the red rain and went over the night's events in his head. Skeeter saw that the moon was still shining bright and the red rain continued coming out of the ground. It covered everything it landed on as it dropped back down. The anxiety of what happened smoldered in his young brain and he finally, after hours of sitting there, drifted off to sleep.

While Skeeter and Rusty slept, the red rain diminished, and the sky filled with clouds that blocked out the moon. A heavy downpour washed away the red hue that tinted the surface of the earth and erased the evidence of what had transpired overnight.

5

WHERE ARE MY STATUES?

The sun rose over Grananite Mountain. It shone down and glistened through the fog. It illuminated the wet dew on the trees just like any other summer morning. The fog lifted, leaving steam on the surface of the earth, and crisp clean air. It started out a beautiful day.

The boys were awakened by the sound of Skeeter's mom screaming, "What is this mess all over the steps?! I thought I told you boys to take your wet clothes off outside last night! Why does it look like blood? Is one of you hurt?"

She ran upstairs to check on the boys. She knocked on the door and then walked in. "What happened to you guys last night? Are you both okay?"

Skeeter's mom startled the boys and woke them out of their sleep. It took Skeeter and Rusty a moment to fully wake up.

"Yeah Mom, we're alright. I don't know what it is. It must be some kind of dye or something. Don't worry. I'll clean it up," said Skeeter as he rubbed his eyes.

Mrs. Copeland gave Skeeter a hug and stated, "I was worried about my little guys. I saw all that blood and thought you were hurt."

"Mom! Don't do that, it's embarrassing," huffed Skeeter as he wriggled to get free from her.

"I don't care what that stuff is as long as you clean it up, and make sure that you do a good job. The house was clean before you showed up and I don't want to have to do it again after you leave. If I need to reclean this mess, I'm going to ground you and I'll make sure that Rusty's mom does the same thing." And with that dire warning, she turned on her heel and charged downstairs in a huff.

Skeeter's mom had long dark hair and was very attractive. She was small, in her late thirties and very physically fit. You could tell she was Skeeter's mom because he was the spitting image of her. She was a very good mom, always attentive to her children's needs, and always involved with some kind of side hustle. When she was not taking care of the family, she enjoyed tending to her rather large garden that helped feed her family. It also supplied the neighbors with vegetables, and it stocked the fruit stand at the end of her driveway. She also did various types of arts and crafts and was a perfect complement to her husband, Skeeter's dad. He worked all day on the farm that had been in the family for generations. She and he shared a good work ethic; one that, on days like this, with reddish mess tracked up the stairs and down the hall, she despaired of ever passing on to her son.

The two boys went out into the hallway, looked at the mess, and saw how they left it.

"Wow Skeeter, it's pretty bad out here. I didn't realize it was like this," said Rusty.

"Yeah, me either. It was dark and I guess we weren't paying attention."

"Why didn't you tell your mom the truth about the red rain?"

"I dunno. I figured she wouldn't believe me if I did tell her. I don't know if I even believe what happened last night at this point."

"Your mom was kinda okay with the mess though. My mom would've probably knocked me silly if she woke up to this."

"No, she wouldn't. She's a nice lady."

"Ha, you don't have to live with her," Rusty commented as they cleaned up the mess. "Boy I'm glad that's over. I don't want to go through another night like that ever."

"You got that straight, Rust. I don't want that to ever happen again either. I do really want to go back and see what happened at the Fortress," declared Skeeter, "so let's hurry up and get this mess cleaned up and we can head back and check things out."

Rusty, even though he was a big boy, had some reservations and was not really willing to go back. He was kind of scared by what had happened. He looked at Skeeter and said hesitantly, "If you want...we can, but I don't know if we should."

"Stop being such a sissy boy. What are you so afraid of?!" barked Skeeter. "What do you think happened over there? If there was a big fire, we would have heard the fire alarms. Nothing happened. It rained all night. I just want to go back and see if we can find that snow globe thingy."

"I think you're nuts, but if that's what you want to do, I guess that'll be alright," grumbled Rusty.

The boys, reluctantly, did a really good job cleaning up the mess in the house. They grabbed their stuff and ran down the stairs.

Skeeter yelled out as they made their escape, "We're done Mom be back later!" The boys ran out the front door, jumped off the porch, and hopped on their bikes.

Skeeter's mom walked out the front door to watch them leave. The boys raced down the driveway.

She hollered to the boys, "Get back here and pick these up!" as she pointed down at the clothes the boys discarded the night before when they came home in the red rain. She also noticed something else missing in her yard.

She screamed bloody murder at the boys. "What did you kids do with all my yard ornaments?!"

She was extremely irate. The mess in the house was one thing, but she had a lot of time and effort invested in her landscaping. To see all of her lawn decorations were gone really got her fuming.

The boys continued down the driveway and heard Skeeter's mom say something, but they were too focused on getting back to the stream to pay any attention to her and just kept going.

Skeeter ignored her and yelled, "See you later, Mom! I'll be right back."

The boys left the driveway, turned towards the stream, and raced up the road, leaving Skeeter's mom to pick up the dirty clothes, confused and angry about what had happened to her yard ornaments.

The boys rode up the road and saw a figure that came toward them on a bicycle. They knew this person all too well.

"Here comes Toots," teased Rusty in a devious voice. "She is fine, finer than a frog's hair split four ways."

"OH! Jeez," Skeeter begged. "Rusty, just this one time, don't start with her. You know you like causing trouble, but all I want to do is go see what happened back at the stream."

The two boys were talking about Alexandria Russo. She was a cute girl with dirty blonde hair and an angelic face, but the one thing that set her apart from her classmates were her beautiful deep blue eyes that resembled crystals. She stood a full head taller than Skeeter and normally wore her hair in pigtails, but on this meeting it hung straight down. All the boys in school had a crush on her, but she only had eyes for Skeeter. She had loved him ever since the time that Skeeter's mom babysat for her and they played together as small children. They were the same age and in the same grade, but they were at a point where the girls develop before boys. The age where girls are young women and boys are still boys. She was maturing into quite a beautiful young lady, but because of his age, Skeeter was not quite interested in any kind of boy/ girl relationship yet.

That's not how Rusty felt though. He was in the same grade but was a year older and was a bit more physically mature than Skeeter. If given the chance, he would surely make Alexandria his girl.

"Hey Skeeter," laughed Rusty in a devilish voice.

Skeeter interrupted and growled forcefully, "I know, I know Alexandria likes me, now shut up."

Rusty always teased Skeeter about the crush that Alexandria had on him, and any chance that Rusty got, he dug at Skeeter about this. Little did Rusty know that every time he teased Skeeter, he inadvertently planted the seed of love in Skeeter's heart. If truth be told, Skeeter liked Alexandria even more than Alexandria liked Skeeter.

"You know why her family calls her Toots, right?" asked Rusty in a petty sarcastic voice, "I was at one of her birthday parties and I heard her drunk uncle teasing her, saying how he nicknamed her Toots because as a little infant she used to fart on him, so he named her Toots and in the family it stuck." Rusty laughed hysterically at himself.

"Shut up," snapped Skeeter, and he punched Rusty in the arm. Skeeter had heard that story a million times and was really sick of it.

All three rode their bikes towards each other and met up in the middle of the road. They stopped and started talking.

"Hi Toots," giggled Rusty.

"Be quiet dogface. You know I don't like that name, and I wish you would stop calling me that," demanded Alexandria, but in a sweet voice she looked over at Skeeter and asked, "Hi Skeeter, where you guys going?"

Skeeter answered, "We're on our way to go check something out."

"Well I'm heading into Roaring Springs. My mom got

a call from Mrs. Carnevali, my neighbor, and she says that we're supposed to stay out of town for a while. There's some kind of chaos going on. She didn't tell us what it is, but if she said we're not supposed to go there it must be something big. I was hoping to run into you Skeeter. I was going to stop at your house and see if you wanted to take a ride in with me and see what all the fuss is about," finished Toots.

The boys looked at each other and curiosity got the better of them. They could always head to the stream later, so they decided to change direction, turned their bikes around, and went with Toots to see what was going on in town.

6

ROARING SPRINGS WILL
NEVER BE THE SAME

The kids arrived in Roaring Springs. It was a small town, a few square blocks wide or so, not like a big city. It had all the essential buildings that a small farming town needed: a drugstore, post office, police station, small library, supermarket, school, and hardware store.

It was just like every average small town in the USA, but when the kids got there, they were amazed at what they saw. There was true utter chaos. It was like a warzone, as if a battle had taken place. The streets were deserted, and everyone had taken cover.

The sheriff and his deputy were in a shootout and they were losing. The standoff was not with a criminal faction, but with statues. Everyday, garden-variety, lawn-type decorative statues that somehow had become animated and were moving throughout the town as if they were alive.

Some of the statues were gargoyles, varying in size from small to rather large. The kids could see that they flew solo at various heights. They soared like birds of prey and with long, slow, precise flaps of their wings they gained enough altitude to circle in search of a victim. It looked as if they moved in slow motion. Once they spotted their target, they tucked their wings tightly against their body and darted from the sky, like a missile from a jet fighter.

Other statues were cherubs. The slower ones fluttered around in large groups, stayed close to buildings and never went too high in the sky, but the faster cherubs moved in smaller packs and seemed to be aggressively assaulting the gargoyles. They kept the gargoyles from reaching the height they needed to strike back. Both gargoyles and cherubs made their way through town, broke windows, smashed streetlamps, and caused all sorts of destruction.

"What's going on here?" cried Toots, barely able to speak. "Why didn't I listen to Mrs. Carnevali? We never should've come into town. This is terrible. I didn't know it was really this bad." She got off her bike and crouched down with her head in her hands and covered her eyes, unable to look at the devastation of what was once their quiet little town.

Glass broke nearby and startled Rusty. He left his bike on the sidewalk, ran over, and sat down next to Skeeter and Toots. All three kids found a safe place to hide next to a brick wall, and watched as smoke and fire came from the windows of the hardware store. The kids had never seen a fire of this scale before and it moved as if it had a life of its own. The slight wind that was generated by the flames made them look as if they were small orange tornados, and they danced like choreographed performers on a Broadway stage as they spread along the rooftop.

"It's gonna be alright," consoled Skeeter as Toots trembled uncontrollably, grasped his hand and refused to let go.

Rusty murmured, "It's not gonna be okay. I'm scared. Let's get outta here."

"I'm afraid too, but Rusty, look at those things. They look like what was inside the Snow Globe," said Skeeter, referring to the gargoyles that the sheriff and his deputy were fighting.

Rusty answered, "Yeah Skeeter, you're right. That's kinda what they look like. You think we did this?"

"Yeah! I do!" exclaimed Skeeter. "I think we did this and we need to do something to make it right!"

"Did what?" asked Toots as she managed to get out a few words through her tears. "What are you guys talking about? I want to know!"

"I don't think we're totally sure what happened last night, Alex. We found something we call the Snow Globe. I read an inscription in it and a lightning bolt came from the sky. It knocked us on our asses and then it started to rain red from the ground. It was really scary. Inside were these gargoyles and cherubs fighting. We were heading to go find it when we ran into you. That's when we came into town and this is where we are now," Skeeter answered. He didn't do a great job as he explained last night's events to Toots. He was shaken up also and left out some pertinent information.

Toots looked confused and puzzled at what she heard and remarked, "Are you trying to tell me that you two were playing and that you caused all this? How? I would never believe a story like that if I weren't seeing what I am seeing right now with my own two lying eyes. Let's say I believe you; what can we do?"

"We were heading back to see if we could find the Snow Globe when we saw you. Maybe we should go do that. I'm not sure what that will prove, but that's a good start, I guess," said Rusty.

Toots calmed down and was no longer hysterical. She came up with a better plan and commented, "We should tell the sheriff about that Snow Globey thing, maybe he'll have a plan what to do."

"Good idea, let's go tell him," replied Skeeter.

The sheriff and his deputy had taken cover between two cars in a parking lot in front of the sheriff's office. They were shooting at the gargoyles. There wasn't just one specific spot in town that was being attacked. It was widespread, all over the place. This was definitely way more than the sheriff and his two deputies could handle by themselves.

The sheriff was big, very big, past the point of obesity. His tall frame didn't carry his excess weight well. He was well over four hundred pounds. His uniform didn't fit anymore. His belly seemed to always stick out over the top of his gun belt. He was definitely a character though, well-respected and loved by everyone in town. He had been sheriff for over thirty years. His weight made him very immobile, but in a town like Roaring Springs, there was rarely any need for a super cop. Sheriff Gara was his name. He was always able to shut down any problems by using his words and never needed to resort to force. When there was a confrontation and he needed a little help, he always kept a couple of tough, well-groomed deputies by his side.

The kids were near the center square fountain, about fifty yards away from the sheriff, and saw him as he took a few shots at the invading enemy. They looked around and noticed that the cherubs outnumbered the gargoyles almost ten to one.

"Skeeter, some of those cherubs are really superfast. One just flew by us and I could barely see it," observed Rusty.

"Is that what that was?" commented Toots. "I felt the breeze as it passed by my head, but I didn't see what it was."

"Come on, let's go talk to Sheriff Gara," insisted Skeeter.

Skeeter and Toots both got on their bikes and rode toward the sheriff. Rusty, too scared to move, sat there frozen. They turned around, looked at Rusty, and went back to give him an encouraging nudge.

"Let's go buddy," begged Skeeter as he pulled at Rusty's arm. "We can't do this without you and we aren't leaving you here."

Rusty looked at his two friends for a few seconds, took a deep breath, and mustered up the courage to move forward.

He jumped up and clapped his hands together to signal he was ready to fight and join in the battle.

All three made their way over to the sheriff. They heard loud bangs, glass breaking all around them, and saw the sheriff as he continued to fire at the gargoyles. The gargoyles were larger, slower, and more docile than the cherubs. The kids approached the sheriff and saw him actually hit one of the gargoyles up close with a shotgun blast. He blew it to smithereens.

The kids got to Sheriff Gara's position, ducked down between the two cars with him, and at the same time said, "Sheriff, sheriff."

Sheriff Gara cut them off. He looked at the kids, pointed his finger for them to go away and snapped angrily, "Get outta here. This is not a safe place for you. I want you to go straight home. Stay there until you hear that it's okay to come out." He and his deputy fired more shots off at the cherubs and the gargoyles that came close to the cars.

A second deputy ran out of the sheriff's office, sat down next to him and reported, "I just got off the phone with the state police and the secretary said I must be nuts. She didn't believe me. She asked what kind of prank is this?! I think you should go in there and try to talk to them yourself. I don't believe we can handle this all on our own, Sheriff."

The cherubs and gargoyles weren't actually attacking the sheriff, deputies, or the kids. They only flew above them in an attempt to pin them down in one spot while others did all the damage, caused mischief, broke windows, and went into the buildings.

"What are they doing?" asked Toots.

"What are they doing? I don't even know what they are! Get out of here I said, you kids are not safe," barked the sheriff at the kids.

"But, but Sheriff, I'm trying to explain to you what happened last night. Why won't you listen?" begged Skeeter.

The sheriff didn't want to listen. He had more urgent problems to take care of and didn't realize that the kids could shed light on what was going on. The last thing he needed was to have three children underfoot. He pointed and motioned for the kids to leave again.

The kids knew they weren't getting their point across. Reluctantly they hopped on their bikes and rode away as quickly as they could. Sheriff Gara and the deputies fired off some cover shots to protect the kids. This allowed them to get away. The sheriff hiked up his pants and ran into his office.

The kids got to the safety of some bushes and watched. They noticed something peculiar. It looked as if the gargoyles and cherubs were actually fighting among themselves.

Rusty commented, "Look, the cherubs and the gargoyles are fighting just like they were in the Snow Globe. That's weird, I wish we could tell the sheriff what we know, but he doesn't want to listen. We need to get that thing."

"You're definitely right, the answer is in the Snow Globe," confirmed Toots.

The kids decided to go back to Skeeter's house and come up with a plan there. They jumped on their bikes and headed home.

While the kids rode, they heard this very strange and weird laughter. It sounded almost like a bunch of toddlers playing. The noise came up from behind and got closer and closer. Skeeter noticed a shadow.

At that moment, Toots was knocked off of her bike by a group of the cherubs. This was the first time that the kids had a good chance to see what they were up against. They got an up close and personal look at the cherubs. They flew around like little chubby babies suspended in midair and flapped their little wings so fast that the kids could barely see them. It sounded like a swarm of bees and they generated wind as they flew around.

The kids continued to hear the laughter of children and this made it hard to think because the cherubs came at them from all angles. They darted back and forth and had the three kids surrounded. The cherubs didn't stand still for one second. When one of the kids got a good look at a cherub it moved away. Skeeter took a quick count and determined that there were about twelve or thirteen cherubs that were attacking them. He also noticed that they looked familiar. Some of the cherubs resembled the statues that were in his mother's yard.

The cherubs continued to swarm, specifically around Toots. Some pulled and picked at her. Others protected the cherubs going after Toots; they acted as backup and kept Rusty and Skeeter away so they couldn't help her. One of the cherubs grabbed Toots's head and pulled her diamond earring off and flew away.

Toots fought the best she could, but it was difficult because these things were very fast, agile, and they could fly. She swung and squirmed frantically. When a second cherub tried to grab her other earring, out of nowhere came a big green flash. It flew through the swarming pack of cherubs that was attacking Toots and made them disperse. When it flew through the swarm it smashed a few cherubs into pieces. This stopped the rest from attacking and they flew away. The green flash that the kids saw was actually an ugly green marble gargoyle.

After the gargoyle scared away the cherubs it flew in a circular pattern over the kids' heads. It seemed to be protecting them. Toots looked at the gargoyle and remarked, "You saved us; those things were going to hurt us, maybe even kill us. Thank you."

It was then that kids realized what was going on. The cherubs, cute baby-faced little innocent-looking figures, were not what they seemed. They were actually evil. The cherubs hurt Toots and tried to steal her jewelry, but the ugly, gnarly, demon-like gargoyle protected her.

"That makes more sense guys," announced Skeeter. He had a "eureka" moment. "When we were sitting with the sheriff, the cherubs were the ones breaking the windows, going in and out of the buildings, while the gargoyles were chasing them. We need to go back and convince Sheriff Gara to stop shooting the gargoyles. He doesn't realize what they are doing. He doesn't know that the gargoyles are good."

That was true. The cherubs were the troublemakers and the gargoyles were the protectors. You would think this would be the other way around—the cute and innocent little kid-like creatures would be nice—but in this case, you would be wrong.

Gargoyles always have been protectors throughout time. They were put on buildings and structures, mostly churches, to protect against black magic and to ward off evil spirits and demons. They've always been misunderstood. People thought because they were ugly dragon-like creatures, they would be evil, but now the kids knew different.

The cherubs moved very fast because they were small and could fly quickly. The gargoyles, on the other hand, were larger, slower, and more lethargic. This was why the sheriff was actually able to shoot the gargoyle, because of their slower speed.

Rusty insisted, "You two go back to the Fortress and try to get the Snow Globe. I'll run back and tell the sheriff what we know. I won't leave this time until I make him understand. I'll meet up with you at your house, Skeeter."

The kids split up, and didn't realize that this may not have been the best idea.

7

MY OLD FRIEND LUCKY

Rusty headed back to town, while Skeeter and Toots made their way to find the orb.

The two kids started to ride, but stopped. They looked back and saw that the green gargoyle had landed, looked at them, and appeared as if he didn't know what to do.

"Let's go Pistachio!" yelled Toots, as she motioned for him to follow them.

Pistachio turned toward them, leaped straight up into the air with his powerful legs, flapped his modest wings, took flight, and followed the two friends.

The gargoyle that the kids were referring to as Pistachio appeared to be very old and carved out of some sort of light green marble. He looked like a yard gnome on steroids. He had big feet, thick legs, very muscular arms, and a face that was not gruesome or pretty, but somewhere in the middle, almost that of a chubby monkey. He had very large ears and a tuft of hair on top of his head. Since he was carved out of marble it was not really hair, it just looked that way. That was how his creator made him.

His wings were not very big, but they were large enough that they could carry his weight as he flew. His hands seemed very large, as if they were able to clobber things well. He carried a pipe of some sort. Some kind of galvanized plumber's pipe it looked like. His feet and hands both appeared to be oversized for his muscular humanoid body. He was no more than three feet tall, about double the size of an average cherub.

"Pistachio?" questioned Skeeter. "Why would you call him Pistachio?"

"I don't know," revealed Toots. "I just think his color reminds me of pistachio ice cream."

Skeeter laughed, shook his head, and the two proceeded on their way as Pistachio followed close behind, as if he was some sort of strange bodyguard.

The two kids rode about a mile or so when Toots stopped and looked off into the distance. She noticed something.

Toots hollered to Skeeter in front of her, "Skeeter stop! Look over there," she pointed. "Is that a group of cherubs? Where are they going? What's in that direction? There's nothing over there for miles."

Skeeter turned back and looked at a group of about six or eight cherubs that flew in the direction of a neighboring town to the west, called Maiden Creek. Since this was a farming community, the next town was well over twenty miles away with nothing between them but farmhouses and open fields.

Skeeter agreed, "Yeah, that's weird. At least they're not bothering us. We gotta get going if we are gonna get the Snow Globe."

"Skeeter, I just remembered something," commented Toots. "Last year when we went to the museum in Paxton City for a field trip, I saw an old ancient scroll sitting under glass in a display case. I couldn't read it, but there was a plaque beside it describing a situation similar to this one. It said that in Rome, the city was terrorized by statues. I'm not sure if it relates to this situation at all, but I figured I'd mention it."

"How is it possible that you can remember something like that?"

"Well, when you and Rusty were running around the halls like little kids playing tag, I was actually there to learn something. And besides, Mrs. Lippencott, the school counselor, told my mom I have an eidetic memory."

"What's that? It doesn't even sound like a real thing."

"It's like a photographic memory. I can retain things I see for a long time. She said a lot of kids have it, but as they get older, they can lose the ability to do it."

"Wow! I always knew you were smart, but I didn't know you were that smart."

"I'm not that smart, I just like to learn."

"Well that is a thought, though. Maybe we should head into Paxton," remarked Skeeter. "I hope it's not a waste of time if we go to take a look at it."

There were not a lot of roads that led in and out of Roaring Springs. As Skeeter and Toots pedaled a little further, they came to a fork in the road. This was a pivotal point in the town's thoroughfare. One direction headed toward the stream and the Fortress area. The other way led to Skeeter's house. Skeeter chose the road toward his house.

Toots sat at the turn, stared at Skeeter, and looked confused. Skeeter realized very quickly that Toots stopped. This forced him to turn around, go back and talk to her.

"What are you waiting for?" inquired Skeeter.

"You're going the wrong way," mentioned Toots, as she pointed down the road towards the stream.

"I know Alex." Skeeter never called Alexandria, Toots. He knew she didn't like it and even though he was not into girls right now, he did have a place for her somewhere in his heart. "I have a different idea. A change of plans. I want to go back to my house and get my brother's dirt bike. We can ride into Paxton and look at that scroll you were talking about. It may be a good idea to see what it says."

While the two kids sat and talked, they both looked up and saw something strange. It was not that unusual considering everything that happened to them today, but on a normal day this would have been pretty bizarre. They saw a gargoyle that was connected to a long, old, thin tombstone as if it were sitting on the stone before it became animated. The poor thing looked crippled. It couldn't fly properly because the headstone was so heavy. It dragged the stone behind itself, came up to the kids, and looked at them as if it needed help.

The two kids just looked at each other and wondered what they could do.

"If we had a hammer I could knock that thing off and I bet she could fly, but we don't have time for that," remarked Skeeter.

Toots, almost in tears, sobbed, "I feel so sorry, I wish we could do something for her. Follow us and we can help you when we get to Skeeter's house."

Not being able to assist the gargoyle, the kids continued on their way toward Skeeter's house followed by their new friend.

BANG! The kids heard a loud noise and glanced back to see that Pistachio had used his metal pipe to free the little gargoyle from her burden. The gargoyle flew a few feet off the ground. She appeared to be unstable, as if the weight of the remaining stone threw off her balance, but with a little practice she looked to be getting the hang of flight.

The new gargoyle was small compared to all the other ones the kids saw. Its paws were fused to small pieces of what remained of the tombstone. She had trouble when she walked, but at least she could fly. Her wings were equal to her length and her body did not have dragon features like the others. She resembled a small, extremely muscular tiger. Her face was cute, but fierce like a cat that was ready to attack, and had two long fangs that protruded from her mouth.

"Wow, look at her go!" exclaimed Skeeter. The new gargoyle flew by the kids extremely fast. "She is faster than the other gargoyles. It must be her size, or maybe because she is a cat. What should we call her?"

"She's covered in moss. She must have spent her life in the shade. Let's call her Mossy."

"That sounds perfect."

Mossy flew ahead of the kids and would stop to smack her paws on the ground to remove the cumbersome chunks of stone. She waited until they caught up and continued with them.

They arrived at Skeeter's driveway and sensed something was wrong.

"Look, Alex, all the windows are broken out of my house!" yelled Skeeter in a frantic voice. "It happened here too. They must have come back when we were gone. I hope my mom isn't hurt."

"I don't see any of them around anymore," remarked Toots, referring to the cherubs.

Skeeter dropped his bike at the step and ran up to see if he could find his mom. He stopped at the door. He didn't want to run in, in case the cherubs were still inside.

"Mom! Mom! You in there?!" hollered Skeeter.

Skeeter didn't get any response. He turned around and saw Toots had a blank stare on her face. She was scared, and pointed up into the open rafters of the front porch. Pistachio flew next to Toots in a protective mode, while Mossy did the same alongside Skeeter.

In the rafters, curled up in a fetal position, was a cherub. It looked almost as scared as Toots. The cherub didn't want to be noticed, but it was too late. The kids already saw it.

Pistachio quickly flew in front of Toots and confronted

the small cherub. He swung his galvanized pipe around in a threatening manner, like a ninja, letting the little cherub know he meant business and not to start anything.

"Wait, don't hurt him. That's Lucky!" declared Skeeter. "He's my favorite cherub. I found him down by that old farmhouse at the stream, near the Fortress. My mom has never sold him because she knows I like him so much."

Skeeter's mom had been making cherub statues out of cement for years. She had a workshop in the barn, with many molds, a cement mixer, trays and dyes. It was a hobby of hers that she was doing to make extra money while Skeeter's dad worked in the fields.

"Let's not be afraid of him," said Skeeter. "He looks more afraid of us than we are of him. He doesn't act like the other aggressive cherubs. I think he is different. If he were like the other cherubs, I think he would've already come after you for the other earring or just have flown off because of Pistachio."

Toots cowered behind Skeeter, scared and reluctant to reach out to Lucky. Pistachio flew guard and wanted to see if Lucky started any trouble.

"Is that true little guy? Do you want to hurt us? Are you like the other cherubs?" probed Skeeter.

Lucky moved forward on the rafter, closer to Skeeter, looked at him and shook his head no.

"Do you want to be friends?" inquired Toots, in a scared raspy voice.

Lucky moved even closer to the kids. Shook his head yes, and started to fly. Skeeter gestured for Pistachio to back up and give Lucky a little space. Pistachio ignored Skeeter's command and continued to fly in a guarded position. He looked through Skeeter and made eye contact directly with Toots. It seemed Pistachio waited to be directed by Toots for instructions what to do.

Toots nodded her head and reassured, "It's okay; let Lucky out. Let's see what he wants to do."

This was the point that Toots realized that Pistachio was her protector, her own personal guardian angel.

Lucky flew down to eye level with Skeeter, directly in front of his face, and made eye contact with him. He was hovering there like a dragonfly. He put his hands together, fingers interlocked, and made a thank-you gesture by motioning his hands back and forth.

"See," asserted Skeeter, "I think he's a good guy and I'm going to give him a chance. He has always been my favorite cherub around here. I remember when my mom was using Lucky as a pattern to make molds so she could create other cherubs. She knocked him off the table one time and I caught him before he hit the ground and broke. My mom said that was lucky, and that's how you got your name little guy."

Skeeter remembered that last night he had seen something out of the corner of his eye. He thought he was seeing things and that it was just his imagination. He realized what he saw was Lucky.

"Was that you last night, in the dark when I came home?" inquired Skeeter.

Feeling more comfortable and less standoffish, Lucky shook his head yes and flew around the porch with the agility of a hummingbird.

"You know what Skeeter? You keep calling Lucky a him, but to me Lucky looks like a she," declared Toots as she looked at Lucky.

"That's what my mom says. She claims that cherubs don't have a gender. They appear as male or female depending on how a person sees them."

"That makes sense. My baby cousin resembles a girl because of long hair even though he is a boy."

Lucky was a little different than the other cherubs. He was not made of cement, like the ones that Skeeter's mom made. Skeeter's mom used Lucky as a pattern and could never get the same detail in her statues as the quality of the artist that

sculpted Lucky. You could definitely distinguish the differences between the cherubs that Skeeter's mom made and
Lucky himself. They weren't as perfect.

Lucky was carved from an off-white piece of marble. He
was rather old, centuries old as a matter of fact. Lucky was
very detailed. He didn't seem to resemble a toddler like a lot
of cherubs do, but was more like an infant. He had a full head
of curly hair and a cloth that draped around his bottom to
keep his modesty. He was chubby like most cherubs were and
his wings were fairly big, almost as large as the span of his
arms. This feature allowed him to fly faster than most cherubs with smaller wings.

Skeeter's mom made a lot of different styles of cherubs, so
not every cherub was fashioned after Lucky.

Skeeter went in the house and looked for his mom. He
couldn't find her. On his way out he saw a note from her on
the refrigerator and read, "I went to find Dad. I'm not sure
what's going on, be back soon, stay safe, love Mom."

Skeeter passed through the garage and noticed that the
station wagon was gone. He needed to move a few things
to dig out his brother's motorcycle. Skeeter was small,
but somehow, he managed to push it outside. He leaned it
against the porch, hopped on and started it. This was not the
first time Skeeter snuck off on his brother's dirt bike.

A dirt bike was primarily used on soil, grass, and off-road
terrain. It was not designed to be driven on the streets. That
was illegal and dangerous because it was hard to handle.
Doing so was a daunting task.

Skeeter looked at Pistachio before he left and asked, "Can
you understand me?" Pistachio signaled yes with a nod. "You
stay here, don't go anywhere. If there's any trouble you take
care of it. Protect the house. You can't follow us because you
can't fly as fast as I can ride. Mossy will keep you company."

Pistachio, like before, looked over at Toots to make sure
that was what she wanted him to do.

She signaled yes.

He knew what the answer would be. He was sad because he couldn't protect the kids as they went on their trip into Paxton City. He realized Skeeter was right and he could never keep up with the dirt bike.

Pistachio looked at Skeeter and gave him a thumbs-up.

Skeeter balanced himself the best he could with his leg leaning on the porch. He asked Toots, "Come get on. You are coming with me, right?"

She jumped on the back of the dirt bike and held on tight. Skeeter ripped off down the driveway and threw pebbles and dirt as he spun the back tire. Lucky followed in tow.

8

THE POWER OF DANTE

Rusty made his way back to the police station. He could see from a distance that in just the short amount of time in which he was gone, the cherub forces had gotten ten times larger. This was a direct result of how Skeeter's mom unwittingly fueled the cherubs' army with her side hustle of all those decorative lawn ornaments she made. She sold these things everywhere: at yard sales, craft shows, flea markets, and even on a table at the end of her driveway alongside her vegetable cart, with a coffee can to collect the proceeds.

Rusty tried to make his way to the police station. Roaring Springs was under a more aggressive attack from the cherubs. Their strength and numbers had grown. They seemed to be more aggressive and in an agitated state. Kind of like a mob rule mentality.

All the people in town remained hidden and stayed out of sight, but Rusty could see some of them as they looked out of their windows.

When Rusty arrived back at the police station, he saw the windows were all busted out. The sheriff's car was gone. He popped his head in and didn't see him anywhere.

A group of cherubs spotted him, swarmed down and attacked. He hopped in the window and made his way to a desk, crawled under and pulled the chair in to protect himself. The cherubs reached and grabbed at him. He saw their angry little faces through the chair. They tugged at it so hard that he needed to hold onto it with all his strength. They had gotten very violent and meant to do him harm. There were twenty or thirty — Rusty wasn't sure, he didn't have time to count them, but he knew there were a lot.

The whole time they poked at him, he heard that eerie childlike laughter that came from the swarm. It was like they mocked him. Rusty knew at this point it was no game. He was scared for his life, trembled with fear, and for being such a big boy his young age was showing.

He thought to himself, *Why did I come back here alone and where is the sheriff?! I need help!*

From under the desk he heard a crash. The cherubs knocked over a filing cabinet, and inside was the town's valuable lost-and-found stash. A collection of jewelry, glasses, purses, wallets, and a combination of all types of things that the people found in town and turned over to the police. When the cherubs saw all the shiny little things, they lost interest in Rusty. They left him alone, grabbed the jewelry and loot, and flew out of the window as if in some kind of trance. Rusty saw all of this and wondered to himself, *What was that all about?* It gave him a chance to try and make a run for it.

He slowly got up and made his way to look out of the broken window. The town was definitely in shambles. He could see that the fire had completely destroyed the hardware store and spread to neighboring buildings. Rusty had no idea what to do. He knew if he could not find the sheriff, he was unable to tell him the gargoyles were good and that they were trying to help. He figured the thing to do would be to head back to Skeeter's house, because that's where they said they would meet. He went outside and cautiously moved toward his bike. Then he heard that ominous laughter.

He thought to himself, *No, not this again. How many more times is this going to happen?* It seemed like there was a lot more cherubs. Their numbers were growing. The cherubs had attacked people all over town. It didn't matter who they were. If on the street, they were in trouble, and now that Rusty was out in the open the cherubs threw their onslaught of violence in his direction again.

Rusty got on his bike and pedaled as fast as he could, but he couldn't get away from them. They seemed like a pack of ravenous dogs, just with the ability to fly. They poked, hit, and smacked him.

Rusty thought, *I wish I had my football gear on. This wouldn't hurt at all.* They finally got the better of Rusty and knocked him off his bike, onto the ground. They continued to pummel him. Rusty curled up into a little ball and pulled his bike on top of himself for protection.

Then out of nowhere came a savior, a warrior, another gargoyle. This gargoyle was twice the size of Pistachio. He was big, very big, the size of a football player.

The new gargoyle flew in and clashed with the cherubs. They were no match for him with his large build. The gargoyle attacked like a wild beast and defended Rusty with all his might. He was able to punch and swat the cherubs out of the air. He even caught one in midair and slammed it into the ground as if he spiked a football after a game-winning touchdown. He managed to take many of the cherubs out. The others knew they had been beaten at this battle, retreated and flew away.

Rusty pushed the bike off of himself, jumped up, and looked at the gargoyle as it flew overhead. The gargoyle took flight to about one hundred feet in the sky. Even up that high, it still looked very large to Rusty. It soared around in a circular pattern to check out the area and made sure that it was clear of all cherubs.

He came back down and landed next to Rusty. He moved and wiggled his shoulders from front to back and side to side. This movement appeared strange, until Rusty realized that this was what the gargoyle needed to do to tuck his wings under each other. The gargoyle looked at Rusty straight in the face. Rusty was not scared anymore. He was safe and the threat had been extinguished.

Rusty looked at the gargoyle. He was old and tattered. Time had taken its toll on him. He was made of cement and it could be seen easily that his outer surface had been weathered by the rain, and his inner aggregate stone, made of various sizes to strengthen the concrete, started to show. Without this inner stone he would crumble.

This gargoyle was large, not short and stout. He was double the size of Pistachio at around seven feet standing straight up. He would tower over most men. He had a very long and lean frame, with muscles that were rippling through his body as if he were a slender bodybuilder, almost like what a track star would have. He was definitely not overweight. His feet resembled hands and his fingers were long and had extremely pointed nails. You could tell he was very strong. His face looked mean, almost like he was a creature of the devil. His forehead and skull had a ridge that came to a small point. It traveled from the bridge of his nose to the back of his neck. He had very long pointed ears and teeth. He almost looked like a vampire or a vampire bat with human characteristics.

His wings were huge and very majestic. They doubled the span of his arms when fully extended. His hideous and gruesome appearance would have scared Rusty to death at any other time in his life, but after this interaction, the gargoyle had shown he was trustworthy and willing to help humans. Despite his appearance he was definitely a friend.

In the casting process his makers added a chain and plaque around his neck. It was his name, and it read "Dante."

"I didn't think I was going to make it. I thought I was a goner. They had me pinned down pretty good, thanks Dante!" exclaimed Rusty in a very appreciative voice.

Rusty felt safe again. He hopped on his bike and rode toward Skeeter's house, but this time he had an escort: his new friend, Dante.

Rusty arrived at the fork in the road where Skeeter and Toots saw Mossy, the one that was dragging the tombstone. Rusty heard that horrifying sound of children's laughter again, but this time it seemed louder, almost like a locomotive was coming at them. Rusty looked back and saw well over two hundred cherubs. They screamed, laughed, and came at him like a runaway truck.

This time it seemed they weren't after Rusty. They were here to attack Dante. They knew Dante was a threat, especially after the vicious beatdown he had given them a few minutes ago.

They hit him with such force that they knocked him out of the air and he crashed to the ground. They piled on him like linebackers after a fumbled football. They pinned him down and they attacked him hard. Rusty couldn't see much of what was going on with all the dust that was kicked up, but he knew his new friend was in trouble. Rusty heard a loud yell and with fury and rage, Dante pushed himself out from under the pile and threw cherubs every which way.

The fight went airborne again and continued for a few minutes. The cherubs regrouped and attacked again. They seemed to be getting the better of Dante. The cherubs' attack style was more refined, more precise. They overpowered Dante and had him beaten back. Rusty tried to help and threw rocks at a couple of the cherubs, but his attempts to inflict damage were futile. All he managed to do was piss them off. Some of them turned their attention towards Rusty. There were way too many. Rusty and Dante couldn't fight against this many unrelenting cherubs. The battle seemed lost. This could be the end.

Rusty used his bike as a shield once again, but then out of nowhere he heard shotgun blasts.

BOOM! BOOM! The cherubs backed off for an instant. Everybody seemed startled, even Rusty. He thought to himself, *Yes, Sheriff Gara is here!*

He looked over and he saw an old truck. He knew that truck all too well; he had seen it in town many times. The cherubs regrouped and began to attack again. They flew in from all directions, attacked Rusty, Dante, and now they had their sights set on the person in the truck.

The person in the truck fired off a few more blasts from the shotgun at the incoming cherubs, knocked them back a few steps, and this allowed him a little time to reach into the truck to get a special surprise for the little troublemakers. He reached in and grabbed a grenade. He pulled the pin and threw it. He didn't want to hurt anyone, so he tossed it about fifty feet away into a field. It was not close enough to hurt Rusty, but the explosion was strong enough to frighten the cherubs away and they fled. Leaving the group alone.

The man yelled to Rusty and pointed to his truck, "Come on boy get in, let's go!" The man in the truck was Mr. McGhee, and for all the trouble and messed up things that Rusty had said or done to this old man, Rusty was sure happy to see him.

Rusty ran for the truck, and Dante followed.

Mr. McGhee hopped out of the truck, raised his shotgun over Rusty's head and yelled, "Get down!"

"Why?!"

"Just get down!"

Rusty did what he was told, and dropped to the ground. He didn't know what was about to happen.

Mr. McGhee fired. This time he didn't have rock salt in the barrel. He shot and hit Dante in the body, wounding him. Luckily Mr. McGhee was using small pellets rather than the full slug, which would have put a nice size hole directly through the gargoyle's body.

Rusty got up and ran up to Mr. McGhee. He begged, "Don't! Don't do that he's friendly he's not the enemy. I'll explain it all to you. Let's go, let's get outta here."

The cherubs started to form up again off in the distance. The swarm looked to see the strange group at the truck.

Mr. McGhee reluctantly lowered his shotgun, not quite understanding the differences between cherubs and gargoyles, but he listened to Rusty and the two got in the truck. Dante followed cautiously, not harboring any ill feelings towards Mr. McGhee. He knew all he was doing was trying to protect Rusty; after all, they had the same goal in mind.

Mr. McGhee told Rusty, "I know you boys have something to do with all this mess that's going on around here. I want to know what you know."

Rusty, in the safety of the truck, began to spill his guts. He volunteered everything that had happened up to that point. He didn't leave anything out.

9

THE MAGIC TOUCH

Skeeter, Toots, and Lucky arrived at the outskirts of Paxton City. The city was about twenty miles to the east of Roaring Springs. Skeeter pushed the limits of the bike, so it only took them about a half hour or so to make the journey. This was a real city, not like the small town the kids came from. It was very big and had many stoplights, car congestion, a lot of pedestrian traffic, police activity, and the normal hustle and bustle that a city of this size created. Roaring Springs, in comparison, only had one blinking stoplight in the center of town.

Paxton City had a population of around twenty-five thousand people. Its footprint on the earth was fairly large, but not as large as a major city like New York or Los Angeles. Its downtown area was packed with brick and mortar businesses and historical buildings. There was an area in the city that was known for its open markets; people from all over the whole region flocked there to buy produce and goods. This was why the city had grown to its current size.

You could see from a distance that the city was set against the majestic Grananite Mountain Range. It was named Grananite because the rock formation was primarily comprised of granite. The mountain range decorated the skyline and stretched for hundreds of miles throughout the region. It gave the whole city a picturesque postcard-like feeling. The majority of the city itself sat mainly in the flat zone at the base of the mountain.

For the most part, the mountain range itself had not been touched by humans because it was basically one enormous granite formation. Its topography resembled a rollercoaster the way the mountain rose and fell, creating its treacherous terrain. The fissures and cracks that riddled every area made it look as if large pieces could fall at any time. Even though it was part of one long mountain range, each summit seemed to have its own personality. Light cascaded differently on each peak. The shadowing created a three-dimensional sur-realistic panoramic effect for anyone who cast their sights on it. To build anywhere on this mountain would be an almost impossible task because of the steep, almost vertical terrain. You could see the rock formations easily because even trees had a hard time living on the mountain. They grew sporadi-cally between cracks and crevasses, and because of the sheer size of the mountain, bushes that covered its surface looked almost like moss that was on an old shed roof.

The Grananite Mountain Range was created billions of years ago when two tectonic plates crashed into each other. This pushed the mantle of the earth out of the ground and up thousands of feet. The government declared the mountain a national park, thus keeping its beauty the same today, as it was when Mother Nature created it so long ago. At the base, however, where Paxton City was built, the area was prime for development. Millions of years had allowed soil to be eroded from the top of the mountain down to the base, and provided lush rich soil and a perfect place for humans to inhabit.

When driving into Paxton from a distance the city seemed small against the mountain, but the closer you got, the more you realized how big the city really was.

Skeeter proceeded to ride down the rural road that led into Paxton City. Up to this point there had not been a lot of traffic, but the closer to the city they got, the more cars there were to slow them down.

Toots tapped Skeeter on the side to get his attention and questioned in a concerned voice, "What are you doing? Are we going to drive the dirt bike into the city? We're going to get caught. The police are going to take away the bike. If that happens, how will we get back?"

"Don't worry about that, I know what I'm doing. I got a plan."

Skeeter cracked the throttle and rode even faster. He had a plan all right. All teenagers know what they are doing. All teenagers have a plan.

In Paxton the two kids made their way through the city. Lucky stayed close, but out of sight. Skeeter weaved in and out of traffic and rode through side streets. He tried to stay in back alleys as much as he could to not be noticed. It was a fairly long way to get to the museum. The kids moved at a quick pace. It was a normal, ordinary Saturday. The streets were busy, cars were moving, people went about their business.

Skeeter and Toots arrived near the museum, around the corner in a back alley. The two kids hopped off of the dirt bike, leaned it against the wall of a building, and Skeeter pushed a small trash dumpster up against it. He tried to conceal it the best he could with boxes, trash bags, and whatever else he could find to hide it.

They did notice something. There was no damage being done around the city. There was absolutely no chaos, nothing bad had happened.

"Skeeter, the city is not being overrun by the cherubs. Look, there are some over there, but they are still just statues," remarked Toots, referring to a restaurant that was using cherubs, sitting on a wall, as decorations.

"I know, right?" confirmed Skeeter. "They must only be alive in our town. Let's go look at that scroll and get back to Roaring Springs."

The kids ran to the museum and made their way to their destination as fast as they could. The whole time Skeeter had told Lucky to stay near and out of anyone's view. He didn't want to draw attention to the fact that they had a live cherub as a companion. They knew exactly where they needed to go because they had been there a few times on class trips.

Upon arriving at the museum, Skeeter looked at the building and took in its architecture as if he saw it for the first time. Skeeter had been here multiple times before, but it was for boring class trips. He had no interest in the museum at that time. He didn't care about it or anything inside. The only thing he cared about before was that he wasn't sitting in a classroom. It was his time to play. He never took his class trips seriously, but this time when he viewed the museum, things were different to him.

The whole world seemed different. It was bigger than just him. Skeeter up until this part of his young life had been extremely self-centered. Everything had to be about him. His wants and his needs—not that he was a spoiled rich kid because he wasn't; he just wanted thing to always go his way. This whole experience had changed him. He felt sad and guilty that the events that were happening in Roaring Springs were his fault, even if he didn't mean for them to take place. He knew he was responsible and needed to do everything in his power to make it right. He stared up at the building, and looked at it in awe.

The museum was huge. It had long stairs that led up to a landing. There seemed to be a hundred steps. You needed to look up from street level to see the top of the museum entrance. Once at the top of the stairs, it appeared as if you were on a mountain peak. The view from this spot was amazing. You could see the Grananite Mountain Range in the distance. It traveled as far as you could see in both directions. It almost wrapped around the city. It was as if the mountain range grew that way. If you looked down from the top, the steps were on three sides. One set of steps was to the left and another, the right. Even the side staircases were magnificent.

Skeeter couldn't understand why he never noticed the beauty of this building before. The facade itself was all the same color. It was made from hand-carved sandstone block, very elegant. The architecture of the building itself was glorious. It had big arched windows that were thirty-five feet tall, with many panes of ornate glass. There were ten huge columns that held up the roof, five on each side of the massive front entrance. The columns were so big that Skeeter and Toots together couldn't put their arms around them. The eaves of the building were adorned with many styles of beautiful molding. They too were cut from the same sandstone as the façade. The roof was green. It was made of copper that had a patina because of exposure to the elements.

The building was incredible. It was a miracle how anyone could have possibly built something like this now, never mind a hundred years ago. It resembled some sort of modern castle.

Skeeter continued to stare up at the building. The experience that the kids were going through had allowed him to appreciate the wonders that man can do. The museum was not as large as the ones in the bigger cities, but for Paxton it was a wonder of modern architecture.

"What are you staring at?" inquired Toots as she gave Skeeter a nudge. "You've been here a lot. We came here every year for the past three years for class, what's your problem? Wake up; we need to get in there."

They made their way to the entrance and then realized something that they weren't prepared for.

"The museum isn't free, we have to pay to get in," blustered Toots in a discouraged voice.

"Oh man, I didn't think of that," remarked Skeeter.

This was a simpler time. Kids never had money on them. Toots and Skeeter weren't rich. Even if they thought about it before they left, they didn't have any money to bring anyway. ATM machines were few and far between and not always available, and they didn't have a bank card if they could find one. You either had cash on you or you didn't. This was going to be a hard obstacle to overcome. They needed to figure it out; after all, they didn't travel all this way for nothing.

They sat there for a while and Skeeter thought of a plan on how they could get into the museum without having money. He hoped it would work

"I have an idea," boasted Skeeter. "Lucky, fly up and sit on the ledge of the museum's roof. Wait there for us; we're going to try something."

Lucky flew up and sat on the eaves of the old museum. The roof had gargoyles on all four corners. They were made of copper. They were cast from a mold and not made of sheet metal like the roof was. They were just sitting there in their normal state, guarding the building. These gargoyles also had a green patina and they all looked exactly the same. They were quadruplets. Each one stood guard over all four corners of the building, like sentinels. If you saw them from a distance they looked like they were small, but when you got up close, they were big, about five feet tall, between the size of Pistachio and Dante.

They were sitting with their legs crossed. They were muscular, but with thin bodies. It appeared that they only had three toes on each foot. A big toe, middle toe, and a pinky toe. Their arms were folded and crossed between their knees. They also only had three fingers on each hand, with no thumb. Their heads resembled that of a goat or ram, more like a ram, because the horns curled back and came forward with the tip at the base of the ear. Their ears stuck up, going through the ram horns. Their foreheads and eyebrows were lumpy, with bumps that went from the bridge of their noses to the tops of their heads. They looked like they were built to ram or head-butt things. Their noses and mouths protruded out of their skull and the lower half of their faces resembled that of pit bulls. These gargoyles were not extremely gruesome like the others. Their wings were not very large; as a matter of fact they appeared too small for their bodies.

"I say we just beg for the money. Let's go back down the steps to the corner and ask people for money. How hard could it be?" grinned Skeeter. "If we ask a thousand people, I'm sure we will eventually get enough."

Toots looked at Skeeter, shook her head in a discouraging way and objected. "I'm not going to panhandle like that. It's embarrassing and it'll take too long. If we have to, I will, but I got a better plan. Follow my lead."

Toots had a very strong head on her shoulders. She was smart and was good at manipulating a situation to get things to turn out the way she wanted. She had a lot of practice dealing with her parents.

Toots walked up to the entrance of the museum and came up with a story. She first tried to just walk in, but when she was stopped by a girl that took tickets she spun this elaborate tale.

"Can we just get in please? We have to do a school report. My mom dropped us off, but she didn't realize we needed money and then she left us here. We just need to get some information for summer school, we won't stay long," lied Toots.

"I can't do that, but wait over here and I'll talk to the curator," said the girl.

While they waited by themselves, Skeeter and Toots refined their story and both got on the same page with the lie they spun. After waiting for a couple of minutes they thought maybe they should just run in. Then came a distinguished looking, tall, elderly businesswoman dressed in a blazer and pleated skirt.

Her skin was flawless and she appeared to not be wearing makeup. She was in her late fifties and didn't hide her age by dyeing her chin-length gray hair that she always had tucked behind her left ear, showing off an ancient earring she was so proud of. She kept her hair shorter because, with the stress involved with her job, it was one less thing she needed to worry about. Late fifties were not elderly or old to those in their fifties, but when you were in your early teens, the fifties were no different than the nineties age wise. Her nametag read, "Ms. Guillebreaux: Curator."

She crouched down to be eye level with Skeeter and Toots and inquired in a sweet voice, "How can I help you two?"

Skeeter couldn't help but notice the perfume that she wore. It had a sweet aroma, like a field of flowers. He couldn't tell exactly what kind they were, but he liked what he smelled. The scent hypnotized Skeeter for a moment while he tried to remember where he had smelled it before. Skeeter looked at Ms. Guillebreaux and thought how stunning she was. He never looked at a woman like this before.

Toots talked with Ms. Guillebreaux, and while she explained, she turned on the waterworks and started to cry. "I...I need to do a summer school report. I thought I could get the information here, but my mom dropped us off. She didn't give me any money because we thought this was a library, not a museum. Now she's shopping, I can't get ahold of her. I don't know what to do!" She sobbed the whole time. That girl could have won an Oscar for that performance.

Ms. Guillebreaux, in a very prim and proper voice, stated, "Here's what I'm going to do: You look like fine children; I will let you in free of charge, but I want you to do me a favor. I need you to give me a copy of the report that you are doing so I can read it. That will be your payment, okay?"

Skeeter and Toots both nodded in agreement and said, "Thank you," and walked into the museum.

❧

Outside, Lucky waited patiently with a bird's-eye view of the city. He sat on the ledge of the museum's roof and tried not to draw attention to himself. He saw two cherubs come at him. They flew up, stared at him, and hovered for a second or two. They motioned with a hand gesture for Lucky to come with them and then they flew away. Those two cherubs had followed Lucky, Skeeter, and Toots all the way from Roaring Springs. Up until this point the war between cherubs and gargoyles had not reached Paxton City.

Lucky saw the two cherubs do something peculiar. One flew over to a cherub statue that was just sitting on a windowsill of a coffee shop and as he touched it, the new cherub statue came to life. This explained how the cherubs' army was multiplying. Somehow the magic that had brought the cherubs to life was passed on through contact, and Lucky saw this.

Lucky looked over at his side while he sat up on the roof. He noticed the gargoyle that was right next to him. He flew over and looked at it. Hesitantly he reached out, slowly, with his pointed index finger. He moved in very close and touched the gargoyle.

Something magical happened. The gargoyle slowly gained consciousness. Lucky had learned a big secret that the cherubs had already known. This secret just might turn the tides of war in our group's favor.

The gargoyle stretched as if it had just woken up for the first time. It reached its arms over its head, yawned and, as it wiggled its tush a little bit, it cracked away from the copper that had soldered it to its pedestal. It pushed off, spread its wings, and took flight. Its wings were not as big as Dante's so it needed to flap them more vigorously to stay in flight. Lucky had a surprised look on his face, seeing the full consequences of what he could do.

Inside the museum Toots and Skeeter found the scroll they talked about, but it was not written in English. The kids read a plaque that hung next to it and this was what it explained:

"This is an ancient scroll written in Latin dating back to the time of 100 A.D. or so. Its origin is not exactly known but it tells a fictional story of a time in Italy involving a sorcerer and how a city was destroyed by statues that had come to life. SPONSORED BY THE GREGORY FAMILY."

"That's exactly what's going on with us!" cheered Skeeter. "I wish we could read that, and the picture that's etched on the plaque looks just like the Snow Globe that Rusty and I found."

"This is definitely related to what's happening; I'm sure of that now. I wish we could take this with us," whispered Toots.

The scroll was sitting on a display rack under glass, on a shelf, hanging on the wall, surrounded by the velvet ropes suspended on brass poles. People would notice if Skeeter tried to grab it, but at that moment, a window broke behind them. It was the cherubs that Lucky had seen.

They broke into the museum, threw stuff around, smashed some of the cases, and grabbed some ancient jewelry. The green Paxton gargoyle, the one that Lucky brought to life, charged through a different window and startled the cherubs. The chase had begun. The cherubs flew off with quick speed in a hypnotic state, and the gargoyle followed. It seemed that once the cherubs had a precious possession, their minds were altered and they switched from aggression to a more relaxed state. They appeared to be pacified, as if the need to hunt for something was extinguished.

Everyone in the museum panicked and ran from the area. During the confusion, Skeeter stepped behind the rope barriers, pushed over the glass case, and took the scroll. He motioned to Toots to get out of there and the two left unnoticed by any of the museum security.

The kids weren't going to wait around to see the outcome of this mess. They ran out of the museum and headed for the dirt bike.

Skeeter looked up for Lucky. He didn't see him. He was supposed to be where Skeeter told him to stay.

Lucky was over watching what the other cherubs were doing when he saw the kids come out of the museum. He flew down and got their attention.

"Lucky, let's get out of here," commanded Skeeter. The kids ran toward the dirt bike. By this time the streets outside the museum were in chaos. People were running, yelling, and screaming everywhere. The cherubs took off around the building and the green Paxton gargoyle followed not far behind.

Lucky knew his new secret. He flew around to each corner of the museum and touched the three remaining gargoyles and brought them to life. Toots watched Lucky and saw the amazing feat he had done.

Since there were not as many cherubs around the city, it was more of a fair fight. Four gargoyles could handle a few cherubs that were in a trance. The cherubs flew away from the museum and looked for a place to stash their loot with the four gargoyles closely in pursuit.

The two kids made it back to where they stashed the dirt bike, uncovered it, and Toots stated, "I bet Father Sarintini will know how to read this. He does mass in Latin." The two kids hopped back on the dirt bike and sped away.

10

RIDE LIKE THE WIND

Unlike when they came into Paxton City, Skeeter didn't hide his presence. He was not trying to be sneaky. He rode straight down the main roads. He swerved around cars and moved in and out of traffic. Skeeter was on a mission: to get back to Roaring Springs and make things right.

He didn't realize it, but he was definitely being a hazard as he rode sporadically and dangerously with no helmet. Toots was on the back and held on for dear life. She had fun coming into the city but at this point she had mixed feelings. Part of her was scared to death, and the other part was filled with adrenaline. She liked the thrill of it.

Skeeter continued to ride down the street. While he passed a group of cars that waited for a stoplight, he crossed the center line and was spotted by the police. He'd drawn the attention of a squad car sitting in traffic on the other side of the road. The cop pulled a U-turn and proceeded to pursue the dirt bike. The cop car was faster than Skeeter, but Skeeter was more agile and able to make tight turns and quick stops. The police turned on the siren and cherries and the chase was on.

Skeeter saw the cop car pull out and started to panic. He could not stop and give up. He did the one thing he could do, his only option, and that was to go on and continue with his journey. If he got caught, there was no way to stop the cherubs from continuing to wreak havoc in Roaring Springs. He knew he had a definite advantage and he began his evasive maneuvers.

There were a couple of patrolmen in the squad car. One of them grabbed the microphone and called dispatch. "We have a visual on the suspects for the APB from the disturbance at the museum. It's a couple of juveniles on a motorcycle heading westbound on Atlas Avenue, we are in pursuit."

Dispatch responded, "Please be advised the suspects are not considered dangerous; they were only seen leaving the area and are just wanted for questioning."

"Copy that," and the police continued the pursuit of Skeeter.

The news of what happened in Roaring Springs was kept to a minimum. The Paxton City Police were only alerted to the trouble at the museum and didn't have any reason at this point to consider that the commotion at the museum and the trouble in Roaring Springs were connected.

The cop car had more horsepower and was faster on a straightaway than the dirt bike. They could keep up with Skeeter with no problem. Skeeter heard the sirens as the car got closer. The quicker the cop car went the faster the siren sounded. Skeeter did some fancy riding, and because the brakes on a dirt bike could stop on a dime, he planned his evasive move.

Skeeter slowed down, moved over one lane, and allowed the cop to pull up alongside of him. At that point he hit the brakes and the cops passed right by. Skeeter then pulled a quick U-ey, went down a side road and lost the patrol car, but because radio signals travel faster than motorcycles, there had been more police called to the chase. Skeeter might have lost one, but three more joined in.

Toots, who before was half scared and half excited, was now completely terrified. She had never been in a police chase and didn't like it. She held onto Skeeter for dear life with her head down and her eyes closed. If there was going to be any trouble, she didn't want to see it coming. Skeeter though, after the initial panic, had calmed down, remained focused, and continued to head out of town.

He looked back and could see three more cop cars chased him. Since this was a dirt bike, he decided to go off-road and made a turn into the city park. The park was a mixture of trees and open grassy areas. There were people everywhere so Skeeter needed to slow down to avoid hitting anyone. The people were also a blessing because they were as much of an obstacle for the police as they were for him.

Skeeter traveled around the park. He moved slowly and meticulously, looking for a way out. He saw it and headed for an opening in the trees. He sped up and used a small hill as a ramp and jumped over a fence, which landed him on a road that went around the outside of the park. The police saw the stunt that Skeeter pulled and radioed for backup to be sent to the road that he landed on.

Skeeter took a moment to regain his sense of direction. He had no idea where he was. He had never been in this part of the city. He knew he needed to travel west so he looked at the sun, put it to his left shoulder, and away he went. His years of Cub Scouts had finally found a practical use in the real world for him. If he traveled this way long enough, he would eventually make it to a road he was familiar with. Toots was not as frightened as before but she was still scared.

The road was long, straight, and didn't have many cars on it, so Skeeter slowed down and tried to be inconspicuous. He passed one car after another with no problems until he was spotted by a squad car that came at him from the opposite direction.

Skeeter thought, *Uhh! I thought I was home free.*

He hit the gas, sped up, and went as fast as he could, hoping he would stay ahead of the cop.

The squad car made a U-turn and sped up to catch Skeeter. It was no accident that the police were on that road. They anticipated that Skeeter might go that route and sent a patrol car to check it out. Skeeter had racked up more charges: speeding, reckless driving, eluding, endangering the public, to just name a few. They were after him for more than just questioning at this point. The police weren't going to just let him drive away.

It wasn't difficult for the police to catch up to him on a road as straight as this one. It was rather easy. Cop cars had so much horsepower. Skeeter had nowhere to go. The road he was on had been cut through a national forest, and both sides were lined with dense trees and a chain-link fence. Skeeter didn't want to give up. He pushed the bike and hoped the engine wouldn't seize. If that happened at this rate of speed, both kids would be goners.

The patrol car caught up to Skeeter easily and was right on his tail. He blew the siren a few times. Skeeter knew he couldn't outrun this officer, but still didn't stop.

The cop spoke on his PA system and gave Skeeter an order. "Stop the bike! You can't get away. There is nowhere for you to go."

Skeeter wouldn't listen. He hoped to find some kind of trail or break in the tree line to get off the road. If he could find that he would be safe, but there was none to be found. If he went on, he figured time was on his side so he continued his course. The cop car stayed directly on his tail and wasn't going to stop either. It was a stalemate at forty miles an hour.

Then a funny thing happened. Lucky, who had been flying above watching everything, came down and flew alongside the patrol car. He kept pace with the cop and knocked on the window to get the patrolman's attention. The cop looked out of his window for a second, saw Lucky, was bewildered, startled and couldn't believe what he saw, but it didn't affect him.

Lucky needed to do something drastic, so he flew backwards like a hummingbird to the squad car's windshield, and looked straight into the officer's eyes. He waved at the cop and this did it. The officer was so distracted and confused that he totally lost control of his car. He swerved and spun out. This caused the car to slide off the road and it got stuck between a couple trees. This unfortunate chain of events — at least for the officer — allowed Skeeter the chance he needed to get away.

Toots looked back, saw the cop had crashed, and yelled at Skeeter, "We need to go back and check on him to make sure he is okay!"

Skeeter was hesitant about going back, but he turned the bike around anyway. The kids pulled up slow and saw that steam came from the mangled front end of the squad car. The cop sat in the open driver's side. When the kids got up close to the officer, he darted from his seat and attempted to chase after them. Skeeter saw this, whipped the bike around and raced away.

"He's okay," reassured Skeeter. They traveled down the road, reached a safe distance beyond the city limits, and were free to slow down. He found a place where he could stop, relax, and decompress.

He hopped off the dirt bike and screamed at the top of his lungs, "We made it!" He was happy that he had gotten away.

Toots didn't share his enthusiasm. She ran up, punched and smacked him in the chest and went into an open rant, "I can't believe you put my life at risk like that! You could have killed the both of us!" She was very irate and continued to browbeat him. A lot of other uncensored thoughts came out of her mouth, with no regard to Skeeter's feelings.

Skeeter expected a different reaction from her since they were safe, but he understood how she felt. He did risk their lives and had no consideration for her feelings.

The two kids settled down, and Skeeter apologized. "Look, I'm sorry. What was I supposed to do? I couldn't let them catch us. We would never make it back to Roaring Springs. Then what would happen? I had to just keep going."

Toots knew Skeeter was right. She calmed down and stated, "I know, it was just very scary. I didn't mean to yell. I was afraid. If we don't get this scroll to Father Sarintini we will never be able to translate it. Those cherubs may grow in number if we don't stop them, and take over the world."

She gave Skeeter a big hug to show him she wasn't mad anymore. The kids had enough time to relax.

"Let's get going Skeeter."

"Yeah, it's time; after all, we have a world to save," boasted Skeeter. He kick-started the dirt bike and pulled out.

Toots leaned forward and whispered in Skeeter's ear, "That was a rush though."

11

OH FATHER HELP US!

Skeeter and Toots made it back to Roaring Springs. They went directly to the church. It seemed like everything in the town had been affected by the cherubs' onslaught of terror. Even the century-old stained glass that adorned the lovely church had been shattered to pieces.

The church was enchanting and charming because of its setting against the backdrop of a forest that led into the Grananite Mountain Range. The church was built within a forest on the outskirts of town. It was a traditional church. The siding was white clapboard and had a dark slate roof.

The front of the church had a big square column with a staircase in the middle of it, which led up to the bell tower. A steeple and cross were on top. The bell tower had two small elongated shutters on each side, making that eight shutters total. The shutters allowed the sound of the bell to emanate, but they did not permit weather to get in. Below the shutters was a clock that sat halfway up between the entrance and the shutters.

The main entrance double doors had a long thin glass window on each side. There were two secondary doors to the left and the right that were exactly the same size as the main door, but arched windows above made them appear larger. The building's body itself was very long with a steep roof which allowed for the open space where the people congregated for service.

On each side of the building there were eight large, arched, stained glass windows. In the rear of the building behind the altar was a particularly enormous stained glass depiction of a Bible scene. The way the stained glass's color caught people's eyes as they drove up to it through the countryside gave the church its unique characteristics. The church itself and its ornate architecture had always been one the most favorite and elegant buildings in the town of Roaring Springs. It was a shame to see that this, the most sacred of places, had been violated by an act of destruction.

"Look at the church," sniffled Toots. "That was the prettiest building in town. Almost all of the stained glass is broken now. Look at it. That's a shame." She placed her hand over her mouth in an attempt to hold back the tears.

"We need to stop this, and stop this now!" fumed Skeeter. "I hope it wasn't a waste of time going to the museum, and that this gives us some answers."

The kids ran around the church and checked all the doors. They wanted to get in to talk to Father Sarintini, but all the doors were locked. They looked in the lower windows that were broken and yelled the father's name, but no answer.

"I bet he's in there somewhere," said Skeeter. "I'm going to climb in this window and look; at this point, what harm could it do?"

Skeeter helped Toots climb in the window. They ran around the church, up the main aisle and yelled, "Father, Father!" They headed down to the basement banquet area where Sunday breakfasts were held for fundraising. The whole time the kids did not make any attempt to be quiet. They made their presence known by yelling Father Sarintini's name. They went down to the basement and headed into the cafeteria. It was a big area which had the same spatial footprint as the upstairs church, but no lights were on.

"This is a waste of time, he's not here," stated Skeeter. Then from out of the shadows jumped Father Sarintini. He held a push broom for defense. He did not wear his cassock, but was in slacks and a sweater. He was dressed like an average ordinary person, but Toots recognized him right away.

Father Sarintini had been the priest at the Roaring Springs Church for what seemed to be forever. Nothing in this town had really changed over the last few decades. Father Sarintini had aged well and being a priest had given him a very healthy lifestyle. Good genes may have played a part in that also. Father Sarintini was of medium height and build. He was clean-shaven and since he was getting on in years, he had white hair.

"What are you kids doing here, what do you want?" Father Sarintini inquired in a stern voice. Being cautious, he was using the broom as a shield to keep the kids from getting too close to him.

"We need help, Father," pleaded Toots.

He realized the kids were not a threat and swapped his aggressive tone for a more calming one and questioned, "What do you need from me Alexandria?"

Toots and her family had been parishioners at the church for as long as she could remember. She was very comfortable talking to Father Sarintini.

"We know what happened to the church. We know what did this," revealed Toots.

In an excited voice Father Sarintini stated, "I know what did this too, I saw them with my own two eyes. It was those little figurines, cherubs I believe is what they're called. They broke into the church through the windows and scared the hell out of me."

The kids stood there, shocked, and giggled. They did not

believe that a priest could say that H - E - double-hockey-stick word.

Toots started to spit out the story of what they had just gone through. "We got the scroll. It tells everything. We were there and Skeeter and Rusty got the ball, lightning strike and these things came to life and started to break everything and I don't exactly know where to start we went to the museum and stole the scroll..." Toots finally broke down from what she had been through and started to cry uncontrollably. Everything that came out of Toots's mouth was total gibberish.

"Calm down, dear. Take a breath and start from the beginning," comforted Father Sarintini, taking Toots in his arms. "Maybe you should tell me the story," and he looked over at Skeeter.

Skeeter started to confess, "Me and Rusty were playing down by the creek—"

Father Sarintini cut Skeeter off. "First son, tell me your name."

"My name is Christian Copeland and I live at 301 Lincoln Road. I like Atari, comic books, riding my bike, candy. I don't like going to school and doing homework and one day I really hope to kiss a girl."

Toots smacked Skeeter upside his head. Father Sarintini laughed and remarked, "Okay son, this is not an audition for a dating game. Let me hear what happened."

Skeeter continued with the whole story from the firework show, to the police station, the museum, and up to the present moment.

"...this is why we are here. We hoped that you can translate this scroll so we can see if there's anything we can do to stop all this madness," finished Skeeter.

Father Sarintini took the scroll from Skeeter and started to look it over.

"My Latin has become very poor," revealed Father Sarintini. "I haven't studied it since I was in the seminary a long time ago." He looked it over. "I think I can do this. I just need to run up and get my Latin dictionary for some specific words."

All three made their way to Father Sarintini's room in the rectory. On the way, they ran into Lucky. He was flying around in the main part of the church where the pews were.

Father Sarintini pulled back when he saw Lucky and started to run down the stairs.

"Wait Father, stop!" shouted Toots. "He's not bad. He's with us."

He stopped, turned around, and was unsure if Lucky could be trusted. After all, the church was destroyed by cherubs and many valuables had been taken.

Lucky also seemed to be a bit uncertain; could he believe in someone that did not trust him?

Father Sarintini was a man of the cloth. He put aside his first instinct regarding Lucky and forgave. "My business is faith. So, I will trust in you kids and give Lucky a chance." He raised his hand to shake Lucky's. Lucky flew down and smacked the father's hand in a high five. He'd seen Skeeter and Rusty do one a few times. That was not exactly what Father Sarintini expected and all four began to laugh, even Lucky. Lucky's emotions started to show. He became one of the group, a trusted member and friend.

They got to Father Sarintini's room. He rolled the scroll out on a desk and started to read it a bit. He looked it over and determined he could make sense of it; not every word, but he got the gist of it.

"Okay kids, I think I have it. Do you want me to read the whole thing or do you want the abridged version?" queried the father.

Skeeter stared at him with a bewildered look on his face and stuttered, "What does 'abridged' mean?"

Toots punched Skeeter, this time in the upper arm, and said in a condescending voice, "That means the short version. Don't you listen in class?"

Skeeter shrugged his shoulders and gave Toots the "what-ever" look.

"Keep going please," said Toots. "Does it say what we need to do? How do we stop them? What do you think Father Sarintini?"

He proceeded to give the kids the shortened version of the scroll and said, "This is a story about how Emperor Tiberius in the city of Rome around 100 A.D. commissioned an alchemist named Gregorius to create a weapon. The emperor needed a weapon to help him take over the world. The alchemist was not only an expert at herbology, the study of plants, but also had extensive knowledge of the full spectrum of metallurgy, the study of metal. He also studied sorcery and witchcraft, which made him a perfect candidate to create such a weapon for the emperor.

"His first attempt was the gargoyles. He thought he could make them come to life. Being hideous, ugly, and mean looking creatures, he hoped they would strike fear, terrorize and wreak havoc on the enemy army. He also knew that being able to fly would surely give the emperor's new weapon a fighting advantage. That was not what happened though. They did not do what the sorcerer thought they would. They only stood guard and protected. It seemed they had no desire to be taught to be destructive no matter what the sorcerer did.

"The sorcerer had a second idea of trying to make creatures that would not be destructive, but become little thieves. He decided to use cherubs. Small, innocent-looking flying beings. He would train these little creatures to fly into the enemy fortresses and hometowns. They were supposed to steal their valuables and bring them back to the emperor. Thus, they would hinder and cripple the enemy's economy and war machine by taking the enemy's resources, like gold, diamonds, silver and coins, pretty much all the shiny little things. With this ill-gotten bounty the emperor could fund his own army, making his stronger, and weaken the enemy's all at the same time.

"It seemed like a perfect idea to the sorcerer, but he couldn't have been more wrong. This also backfired on Gregorius because the cherubs did not distinguish between the enemy's and the emperor's subjects. They attacked the city that the emperor was trying to protect. The cherubs waged war against the wrong people, the people they were developed to serve. The city was torn apart by the cherubs. It also says that there was a struggle between the gargoyles and the cherubs. The gargoyles were natural protectors and tried to stop attacks by the cherubs. It says here that the battles for Rome went on for weeks and weeks." Father Sarintini looked up at Skeeter and Toots and questioned, "Do you want me to continue?"

"Yes, yes."

The father continued, "Gregorius knew that the idea of a weapon like this was bad, especially after witnessing the devastation and destruction that the cherubs had done around the city for the past few weeks. He decided to put an end to it. He conjured up an energy ball through his infinite wisdom and ancient powers. Somehow, he placed a spell of magic on the sphere and when the crystal ball was complete the sorcerer spoke the magic words in Latin, 'sit eos somno' which means 'let them sleep.' The sky opened up and red rain fell from the sky on all the statues that were alive, and they became inanimate objects once again, and the city was back in order."

"So that's what we need to do," announced Skeeter. "We need to go to the Fortress and get the Snow Globe, like we were supposed to do in the first place."

"Yes, that's it in a nutshell. You get that crystal ball and read the phrase and, according to the story, this will all stop. The secret is in how the spell is read. The magic command, or banner that is flying inside the Snow Globe, depends on the state of the statues. If they are alive, the banner will tell you how to put them to sleep. If they are asleep, the banner will tell you how to wake them up. The banner is always changing. It is like a light switch. You can turn it on and off.

"It also says that Emperor Tiberius was so embarrassed about the tragic events that went on in the city that he had all records destroyed that confirmed the existence of living statues. Over time, without evidence the whole story was covered up with lies and quickly became a fairytale and never made it to any history books."

Father Sarintini didn't want to scare the kids, but the scroll also told how the red rain was actually traces of concentrated human blood that was spilled over millennia. It was saved in the soil and released by magic; that was why it came up out of the ground when the incantation was read. The blood gave life to the statues when it touched them.

He stopped summarizing the scroll because the kids had the information they were looking for, but there were other pertinent pieces to the story that he didn't get to tell the kids about.

"Well, it wasn't a waste of time going into Paxton for the scroll. Even if we went and got the Snow Globe first, we wouldn't know what to do with it," said Toots. "Thank you so much Father Sarintini, you were a big help." Toots went over and gave him a big hug and the two kids ran out.

"Wait!" shouted Father Sarintini. The kids stopped and turned around. "May God look over you and guide you in your journey to right this wrong that has overcome our little town." He made the sign of the cross and blessed the two kids.

"Thanks, Fadda!" the two kids yelled in unison, and they turned around and ran out of the room.

12

LOVE'S FIRST KISS

Skeeter and Toots made their way from the rectory and to the window of the church that they originally came in, where they'd left their bikes. Toots looked out and realized it was higher than she thought and didn't want to jump. She turned around and looked at Skeeter.

"What are you eating?" Toots questioned with a bewildered look on her face.

"They're crackers. I found bags of them next to that knocked over cabinet," answered Skeeter as he pointed to a cabinet that the cherubs had tipped over as they looked for loot. "You want some?" and he offered her the opened bag.

"No, those are communion wafers. You're not supposed to be eating those; you gotta go put them back! I think that's a sin!" snapped Toots.

There stood Skeeter, eating out of the bag like they were potato chips.

"...but I was hungry," mocked Skeeter as he shoved the rest in his mouth.

It was not a sin to eat them like that, unless they were blessed by a priest. Since they were not, Skeeter's eternal soul was still safe, at least for only eating communion wafers because he was hungry.

Skeeter hopped up on the windowsill, jumped down, turned around and reached up, ready to grab Toots as she jumped. Toots jumped and her momentum caused Skeeter to fall down on his back. She fell on top of him, looked down directly into his eyes, smiled, moved her head in closer to his. Her long hair hung down the sides of his face.

She moved her lips towards his and proceeded to give Skeeter his first real boy/girl kiss. This was no sister's peck or a grandma's smooch. This was a real boyfriend/girlfriend kiss and lasted a very long time. Toots knew this was probably the only opportunity she would have like this. So, she went for it.

Lucky was flying above the two and became embarrassed at witnessing their first kiss. He started to blush and chuckled as he turned away, so as not to invade their private moment.

Skeeter definitely didn't expect this to happen. He got a tingle down his back and a shiver up his spine. He never felt this way before and he sure did like it.

That magic worked on Toots also. She got butterflies in her stomach and she could feel the hair stand up on the back of her neck. She kissed the boy of her dreams and knew she wanted to spend the rest of her life with him.

Toots finally let Skeeter up. When the two were on their feet, she gave him a big hug and nearly squeezed all the air out of him.

"Okay, now that we have that out of the way," giggled Toots, "we need to get our heads back in the game."

Skeeter tried to talk, but nothing came out. He nodded his head in a goofy way and not knowing what to do, he awkwardly put his hand up in the air and gave Toots a high five.

The two kids jumped on the dirt bike. Toots held on tight, tighter than she did before. She couldn't believe she just gave him a kiss and her head was filled with happy thoughts, even after everything that had happened. She knew this would be the best day of her life.

Dummy, dummy, was what Skeeter thought. *She gave me a kiss and I gave her a high five. She must think I'm a real goofball.* Skeeter's head was all over the place. He had to shake himself out of this and get back in the game like Toots said.

Skeeter rode fast, as fast as he could. He went through the town, down to the fork in the road, and made it to the Fortress. Skeeter noticed that the place looked a little different during the day than when they had left last night. It was not quite as closed in. It seemed more open.

He also saw that there was evidence of a vehicle being there, because in the low-lying areas where there had been standing water, there were deep ruts and a spot where the vehicle turned around and drove back out. The ruts definitely were not there last night.

The two kids raced to the burned-up area where the Fortress stood and Skeeter looked down, trying to find the orb. All he noticed was footprints that tracked up the whole area. It looked as if there had been someone there for sure.

"Who could have been here?" inquired Skeeter. "I don't see the Snow Globe anywhere. What are we going to do now?" He searched frantically.

"We need to keep looking. If we don't find that thing, this whole situation will be hopeless," murmured Toots in a desperate voice.

The kids looked for a while. Skeeter stuck his hands into the mud around the area where he thought he dropped it. Who was to say for sure where he was standing? He couldn't remember exactly but believed this was the spot. There were too many new footprints in the mud to be sure where he was when he let go of it. He couldn't find it.

"We need to get out of here, somebody else has got it. Maybe we can find who was here in town," remarked Skeeter.

Once again, the kids hopped on the dirt bike and rode

away. They drove about half a mile when the engine of the dirt bike started to sputter and died. The dirt bike ran out of gas. Skeeter jumped off looked down and moved the gas valve to reserve. He realized at that point that the gas valve was already on reserve and he had used it all up.

"How could I have been so stupid? We don't need this right now," Skeeter huffed in a disgusted voice. "We don't have the Snow Globe and we ain't got no gas. Okay, Mr. McGhee's barn is over in that direction. I bet you he's got gas somewhere. Let's go look."

The kids walked at a very fast pace back past the Fortress and along the path to Mr. McGhee's house. At times they picked up the pace and even ran.

Skeeter helped Toots get through the barbed-wire fence that led to Mr. McGhee's backyard. They looked up and saw that Mr. McGhee's house had been broken into also.

"Well, even Mr. McGhee's house is busted," mentioned Skeeter. They moved in cautiously and looked for a gas can. Then they heard the laughter of children.

It seemed like the cherubs had some sort of telepathic communication, like bees or insects, because when one was alerted, they all got alerted. The cherubs were be able to group together very quickly. A pack formed and flew down toward the kids. A few buzzed by Toots's head and tried to snatch her remaining earring. Others were after Skeeter, while Lucky picked up the nearest thing that he could find: a fireplace poker that Mr. McGhee used to tend a fire pit in his backyard. Lucky used the poker like a sword to fend off the cherubs. He did the best he could to give the kids some time to get inside.

They ran and took shelter in the house. Toots headed straight upstairs. She thought Skeeter was right behind her, but he tripped, fell, and rolled along the floor. He ended up under the kitchen table. The tablecloth kept him out of view.

The cherubs saw Toots as she ran up the stairs, made the turn around the corner and down the hall. They pursued her and missed the fact that Skeeter rolled under the kitchen table. The cherubs' full focus was only on Toots. She made it into the bathroom, closed the door and locked it. The lock was not very strong. It was old, the kind operated by a skeleton key. The door itself was made of solid wood and was built sturdily. The cherubs worked on busting down the door. When that didn't work, they tried to punch through the wall. This was hard to do because these old farmhouses were built using plaster and lath and not paper-thin drywall, like houses are today.

Skeeter heard the commotion upstairs and knew he needed to do something to help Toots. He looked around and the only useful thing he saw was a medium sized cast-iron skillet. He grabbed it and made his way upstairs to the second floor, where he heard the banging of the cherubs as they violently ripped and tore at the solid wood door to the bathroom. Skeeter rounded the corner at the top of the stairs; at that point the cherubs made it through.

Toots hid in the shower, curled up in a ball. The only thing that protected her was a shower curtain and the toilet scrub brush she had in her hand. She shrieked in a high-pitched voice and yelled for help.

Skeeter ran into the bathroom and swung wildly at the cherubs. The cast-iron skillet seemed to be a fairly good weapon because of its broad surface, and it was easy to wield. He knocked a few of them into pieces. He hit one, but only broke off its lower half. The cherub still had a head, arms, and wings. It continued to fight Skeeter. If this were not such a serious situation, it would have been comical.

The cherubs switched their attention from Toots to Skeeter. He was a bigger threat. They all came after him. He ran out of the bathroom leading them down the stairs and away from Toots. He hoped they would follow him outside where he had a better chance to defend himself, but he never made it. They chased him down and tripped him up before he even got to the front door. The cherubs sensed something different about him—maybe it was because he once had possession of the orb—but they seemed to only focus on him.

Toots could finally get out of the bathroom. She darted out of the house and sprinted down the driveway. She saw someone as they drove up.

It was Mr. McGhee, Rusty, and all three gargoyles. Dante, Pistachio, and Mossy were flying above the truck in a V formation. This was Skeeter's own personal cavalry.

"Hurry, they have Skeeter in the house. They are hurting him!" screamed Toots.

Dante flew into action first, Pistachio second, and then Mossy. Some of the cherub swarm heard the truck pull up and came out of the house ready for a fight. Dante engaged the first group and they led him up into the sky, and a ten-on-one fistfight happened at forty feet off the ground. Pistachio was busy with the rest. He swung his pipe like a major league slugger and knocked cherubs into pieces as each came up to him.

Mossy had her own unique style of fighting. She was the same size as most cherubs, so she couldn't use brute force to overcome an enemy. She had figured out a special trick though. When one flew up to her, she grabbed it with all four arms, gave it a bear hug, and this would take them out of the fight. Since she was catlike, she was always able to land on her feet. She rode the cherub that was in her arms down and at the last moment she would use the cherub's own weight against itself and slam it into the ground. This pulverized the cherubs most times.

Rusty and Mr. McGhee went into the house while the gargoyles kept the cherubs busy outside.

Skeeter was pulled deep inside the house. Rusty heard the commotion and headed in that direction. He made it to the living room where Skeeter was taking a beating. Rusty saw Lucky as he tried to defend Skeeter the best he could, but there were too many for him to make a difference. Rusty was armed with a baseball bat and helped Lucky. Mr. McGhee was not far behind and was the reinforcement that was needed to stop the vicious assault on Skeeter.

With their numbers cut way down, the remaining cherubs retreated. They regrouped outside and flew away as the eerie laughter started to fade into the distance.

Everyone's concern for Skeeter turned to a sigh of relief when they got to him. He was beaten, bruised, and scraped up, but for the most part he was okay.

Toots gave Skeeter another hug and Skeeter sighed, "That was a close one. I'm just glad you didn't get hurt Alex."

"I'm glad you came when you did, Mr. McGhee," rejoiced Toots, and then out of nowhere Skeeter ran up to Mr. McGhee, threw his arms around his big fat beer belly, and gave Mr. McGhee a hug and started to cry.

Skeeter trembled, and in a very soft, sad, and meaningful voice said, "I am so sorry for all the times we crossed through your yard and caused trouble for you." Skeeter wept and you could tell this was a true, heartfelt, meaningful apology.

Mr. McGhee put his hands on Skeeter's back, pulled him tight and consoled, "I know that kiddo. I was young once, and I know boys will be boys." Mr. McGhee may not have forgotten all the things that the kids did to him, but he was willing to forgive. This wasn't the time to hold a grudge. They had bigger problems to take care of.

"I know how to stop all this," Skeeter declared. "We went to the museum and got an old scroll. We had Father Sarintini decipher it. All we need is the Snow Globe. If we read what's on that floating banner thingy, it should stop all this. But we went back to the Fortress and we couldn't find it, and without that, this could go on forever or until we destroy every cherub."

"That's okay Skeeter. Mr. McGhee and me went back to the Fortress and we have the Snow Globe," assured Rusty.

"Where is it? Give it to me now so we can stop this," requested Skeeter.

"I don't have it here. We said we were going to meet at your house and I was afraid I would lose it, so I stashed it there," reported Rusty.

"It's all right boys. We will get back to Skeeter's house, get that ball, and we'll put these little vermin back where they belong. Everybody get in my truck and wait there," commanded Mr. McGhee. He went into his house, grabbed a duffel bag and a few more swinging weapons, including a baseball bat and axe handle. He came out and threw the bag on the floor of the truck, turned it around and spun the tires down the long gravel driveway, and they left for Skeeter's house.

13

IT'S GOTTA BE OUR LITTLE SECRET

The kids sat on the bench seat of Mr. McGhee's truck and chanted, "Let's get the Snow Globe! Let's get the Snow Globe! Let's get the Snow Globe!" as if they were at some kind of pep rally or it was Christmas day and they were going home to unwrap their favorite presents.

Mr. McGhee listened to them sing with excitement and thought, *Oh boy, what did I get myself into? I'm a grown man driving around with juveniles*, but then he realized that the kids had been through a lot and so had he. They could have a moment of happiness without being judged, so he joined in and they all rejoiced because this would be over soon.

The ride from Mr. McGhee's house to Skeeter's was not a very long one. It did take some time and had been uneventful because Pistachio, Dante, Mossy, and Lucky flew outside, flying shotgun to protect the truck.

The kids quieted down and Rusty looked at Mr. McGhee and questioned, "Why don't you tell Skeeter that story you told me about last night and the lightning strike?"

Mr. McGhee nodded and started the story. "I was watching TV and I could hear you kids off in the distance shooting off your fireworks. I was about to come out and see what you two were up to but I was really involved with my program on TV, and didn't want to bother with walking all the way out there. I figured if you got hurt, you would come running for help. I knew you guys were down at the old Gregory foundation and were far enough away from my property that it didn't matter.

"When I heard the lightning strike, it sounded like it was right in my backyard. I jumped up from my seat, ran to see what it was. I knew it was a clear and calm night, and there was no rain in the forecast. I threw on clothes, put on my boots and went outside. That's when I heard you two yelling, and I noticed the red mist coming up from behind you, or at least that's what it looked like to me. I felt it was odd because there were no clouds in the sky and the moon lit my yard. I watched as you guys stopped at my fence and climbed through. You didn't notice me but I saw you both. You two are lucky it wasn't raining hard yet and you didn't rip up my yard. If you did, you would be in real trouble now," joked Mr. McGhee.

He laughed and continued. "From my vantage point, the red mist was following you two. As you slowed down, it slowed down, and as you sped up it sped up. Wherever you were it stayed with you. That's how it looked to me, from a distance. The mist eventually turned into heavy red rain and it came from out of the ground. It spread out in a circle from the point of the lightning strike to where you two were. Basically, as you moved, it followed you. I also noticed that when the red rain hit all those little figurines—the ones my wife got from your mom, Skeeter—they came to life.

"I couldn't believe my eyes. I was in the greatest war of all time and have seen a lot of messed up things in my life that you kids would never believe, but when those statues started to move, that was one of the most incredible things I have ever witnessed. I wasn't sure what I should do. It was like some kind of scene out of a fairytale, or horror story."

Mr. McGhee continued his story. The kids listened as if it were a campfire tale. "Those things came to life and immediately broke into my house through the windows. They weren't attacking me at first; they just started breaking the windows, flying around, and rummaged through all my stuff. They were definitely looking for something. I felt my house was under attack, so I grabbed my shotgun and started shooting those little buggers.

"Once I started shooting them, they began defending themselves and attacked me. I was able to hold my own but not before they grabbed most of my wife's jewelry, her collection of silver spoons, some other sentimental objects, and they even tried to take my gold tooth. They looked like they had enough and fled off. The whole time they were assaulting me and my house there was this childish laughter.

"I spent all night waiting for them to return; I could hear when they did come back. The laughter gave them away. I would pick them off one by one like I was shooting skeet. They seemed to know I was killing them. They got smart and left me alone at that point. They already got most of the important stuff from me. My wife loved her silver spoon collection. She always said she wasn't born with one in her mouth, so she just had to buy them. She purchased one every time we went on a trip somewhere in the gift shop. I made that box she kept them in with my own two hands." Mr. McGhee's voice had gone into a somber tone and it almost looked as if he were going to cry.

The kids just sat there, and did not know what to do or think. Here was this big burly looking man and tears ran down his face.

"Mr. McGhee, what did you call that old farmhouse, the broken-down stone one down by the stream? Whose property did you call that?" questioned Toots.

Mr. McGhee said, "Gregory was the name. Fifty years ago, I bought my property from his grandkids. This whole area was the Gregory estate at one point. He owned everything for miles. The story was that he built his house next to the stream not realizing it would flood every couple years. Every time it did, the inside of his house was destroyed, and he would rebuild it. No one understood why. When he died his family sold it off."

"Skeeter, did you hear that? That was the family's name on the plaque. The one that donated the scroll to the museum. Father Sarintini said the name of the sorcerer who conjured up the Snow Globe was Gregorius?" remarked Toots. "I wonder if the Gregory family were descendants of Gregorius."

"I don't know," replied Skeeter, "but I guess it could be possible. I did find Lucky and the Snow Globe in that area. I wonder what else is there."

"...and I'd bet he was crooked, and that's how that old man Gregory had enough money to buy all this land back in the day. He probably was able to use the Snow Globe to rob people," complained Rusty. "I bet he was more rottener than a five-week-old bananar, sittin' underneath Grandma's bed." Rusty had no idea of what Mr. Gregory had done in his life—none of the gang did—but Rusty had always been cynical and thought the worst of people.

The rest of the ride to Skeeter's house Toots told the story that was written in the scroll about how the orb was created.

"Okay, we now know what we need to do," reassured Mr. McGhee as they neared Skeeter's house. "We need to get to that Snow Globe, read the incantation, and when this is all over, we don't mention to no one you guys did this. If Roaring Springs ever knew this was your fault, you would never have any peace. Believe me I know that from personal experience. It's gotta be our little secret, swear."

"We swear," the kids vowed.

Mr. McGhee knew that would never happen. There was no way a secret like this could stay underwraps. There were too many variables. It would be just a matter of time before someone blabbed—one of these three kids, Father Sarintini, or someone in the sheriff's office. The only hope the town had was to confine it and shut it down as soon as possible. No one really knew how long this could go on if they didn't.

Mr. McGhee pulled up to Skeeter's house and they saw an unbelievable sight.

14

CAN YOU FEEL THAT?

The group made it halfway up Skeeter's driveway and stopped. They could see from a distance that there were thousands of cherubs, *everywhere*. Some were sitting on the house and barn, in the trees, and some were flying. They acted as if they were looking for something. They must have been able to sense the orb was on the property somewhere. If the cherubs found the orb, the incantation to stop them could not be read and the cherub army would continue to grow stronger.

Mr. McGhee reverted to his days in the military during World War II and said, "We can't just rush in there and try to grab that thing. There are way too many of them. We have to come up with a plan, a diversion; a distraction. Somehow, we need to get them to move. We need a strategy. Where exactly did you put the Snow Globe, Rusty?"

"I didn't really hide it. It's in the barn, on the wheelbarrow, sandwiched between two bags of cement," answered Rusty.

"Okay," planned Mr. McGhee, "we need to make a diversion. Something to get these vermin to move. I'm thinking we may need to go find more jewelry. Something to lure them away, but where can we get it? Do you guys have any plan?"

"Wait a minute," interrupted Skeeter. "Remember that cemetery, Rusty? The one that's behind your house, Mr. McGhee. I was looking at some of the tombstones when we were there before, and I noticed through all the brush and thicket that there were gargoyles on the gravestones. If we drive down there, maybe Lucky can bring them to life. Those gargoyles can help us fight these cherubs. I'm not sure how many there are but it's a thought."

"That's probably where Mossy came from Skeeter. She was dragging the headstone behind herself," reminded Toots.

"Yeah, I think you are right, but the red rain had fallen on them. Wouldn't they already be alive?" questioned Rusty.

"Not sure," commented Mr. McGhee. "It may be worth a shot. Couldn't hurt to look. It's not far." Mr. McGhee thought about this and pondered for a moment.

While they were talking about what to do, the cherubs got restless and almost every one of them started to take flight. They seemed to be spooked that the truck pulled up. There were so many of them that they were blocking out the sun. A few of them started to swarm round the vehicle. Dante, Lucky, and Pistachio went into guard mode and were able to protect the truck for the moment. Mossy was not much of a help when it came to the defending department so she just hung back. Pistachio and Dante would pick them apart if they attacked individually, but there was no way the three gargoyles and Lucky could stop that many cherubs if they decided to make a full-blown attack on the group.

The cherubs just waited to see if the boys would show them where the orb was.

"It looks like they know that the Snow Globe is at your house," pointed out Toots. "Why else would they all be hanging here?"

"How could they possibly know that it's here?" asked Mr. McGhee. "They do gather together quickly when one senses something. I wonder if they have some sort of extrasensory perception."

Skeeter paused and went silent for a moment. Then he stated, "It's weird. I know it's here too. I don't know where exactly, but I can feel the energy from the Snow Globe. I can't explain how I feel it, but I do. Can you guys feel that?"

"I don't feel nothin'," said Rusty.

Toots shook her head no also and Mr. McGhee asserted, "That may be why they are here. They feel the same thing as you do Skeeter. Let's go see if we can get reinforcements."

Mr. McGhee pulled away and headed down the road that led to the cemetery. He drove on the path that went through the field. It was not quite wide enough for the truck, but he seemed to manage. It was bumpy and they bounced around a lot.

A portion of the cherub swarm followed and stayed close enough to observe the truck's movements. The nearer they got to the cemetery, the better Mr. McGhee felt about the plan. His memory started to come back.

"I forgot all about the cemetery. It's been years since I had even seen it and it was overgrown then," remarked Mr. McGhee. "I remember that when I bought the farm, the cemetery was more open and there were a lot of gargoyles around it. I can't believe I didn't think about this first."

They arrived at the cemetery. A majority of the cherubs watched from a distance. Dante and Pistachio stood guard. Mr. McGhee and the kids cautiously got out of the truck. They saw that it was a tough job to get through the thicket and over the barbed wire.

Toots yelled in an excited voice, "Look, there are some gargoyles in there! This is gonna work. We have the extra help we need."

Mr. McGhee noticed, "Wow, this has grown so much more

than I remember. The vines are so thick I can barely see the gravestones anymore. That's probably why the red rain didn't activate all the gargoyles."

"You know the plan Lucky? You fly in and touch those gargoyles. Bring them to life. Let's get them involved in this fray," announced Skeeter.

Lucky nodded yes and flew off.

The gang's hopes were high, that this could be the plan that helped swing the battle in their direction. Lucky flew carefully over to the cemetery. He noticed he was not going to be able to just fly in and touch all the statues directly. The bushes were too dense. He needed to climb down like a monkey to reach most of them because of the impenetrability of the trees and vines. There was no need for anyone else to try to make it through all the overgrowth. They couldn't do anything even if they got there. This was something Lucky needed to do on his own. He made his way through the trees. He climbed down and was about to touch the first gargoyle statue. He extended his hand, and pointed his finger.

The cherubs that watched from a distance realized what Lucky was doing and sensed the impending danger. The swarm of cherubs, which was half of the army that was at Skeeter's house, was well over five hundred, and flew into the thicket like a steam locomotive. There were so many of them that they made it through the overgrowth easily. They smashed all the lifeless gargoyles in a preemptive strike to take out the enemy before they could be a threat. The gargoyles that did happened to become enlivened by the cherub's touch were immediately beaten to a pulp. They never stood a chance. It was total devastation. Not a single gargoyle survived.

"Oh! Look at that!" screamed Toots. "Lucky is in there! He's never going to make it out alive! Look at what they're doing Skeeter!"

"I don't know what we are going to do now. Those things

are destroying every tombstone. They're not leaving a single one standing!" cried out Rusty.

"Look there's Lucky, I see him!" cheered Skeeter.

Lucky escaped the mayhem and flew straight up out of the dust like a rocket ship.

"Look he's okay! Hurray!" Toots pointed. Lucky flew away from the danger. A few of the cherubs chased after him, but with his larger wing size and being a cherub himself, he was able to fly faster than they could. "He got away."

"Hurry! Everybody back in the truck," ordered Mr. McGhee. The mob of cherubs had set their destructive might toward the truck.

Toots leaped in the driver's side door and scooted over. Mr. McGhee hopped in next to her and the two boys jumped in the bed of the truck. Mr. McGhee saw they were in and pulled away.

The cherubs gained on the truck and tangled with Dante, Pistachio, Mossy, and Lucky. They held off the cherubs the best they could, but it wasn't good enough. They were overtaken by the huge surge and all vanished in the mass of angry cherubs. The cherubs caught up, banged and smacked at the truck. The boys were tucked down as close to the front of the bed as they could get so the cherubs wouldn't hurt them. Mr. McGhee opened up the sliding back window of the truck, told Toots to hand his duffle bag to the boys and said, "You two know what to do with these."

The boys opened up the bag, peeked in, and a look of excitement came across their faces. They knew exactly what to do.

Skeeter put his head in the window and said, "We can't light them though."

In the duffle bag were some very large fireworks that Mr. McGhee had been saving for a special occasion. They were huge and not like the little ones the boys played with at the creek battle. They were over three feet long and had a lot of power.

"Open the glove box and give Skeeter the flare," Mr. McGhee commanded Toots, and she did what she was told.

Skeeter took the flare, lit it, and handed it to Rusty. Skeeter reached into the bag, pulled out a large bottle rocket, and held it for Rusty to light the fuse.

It burned down and at the last second Skeeter tossed it at the cherubs. The rocket took off and disappeared into the crowd of cherubs.

"That didn't work!" exclaimed Rusty.

"Do it again!" yelled Mr. McGhee, and the boys continued to fire multiple bottle rockets at the cherubs, but they just whizzed by. Skeeter was almost out of ammunition. He lit one, held it down like the others, and at the last moment he threw it like a bowling ball with an under-arm swing. The rocket took off, but one of the first cherubs behind the truck caught it miraculously and turned it toward the boys. Before it flew back, it exploded and blew a big hole in the mass of cherubs. It made them scatter.

Skeeter lit another and prepared to toss it when he noticed the cherubs backed off of their pursuit because the last explosion startled them. Skeeter threw it anyway and it flew at the cherubs and exploded like the one before. That did it; the cherubs must have had enough. They gave up and allowed the truck to drive away. The boys saw all the cherubs stopped in place and look at them. They hovered for a bit and then flew off straight in the direction of Skeeter's house over a farm field.

Dante, Pistachio, and Lucky caught up to the truck, but Toots looked back and shouted, "Where is Mossy? I don't see her!"

Mossy was gone. With all the commotion no one noticed what happened. The cherubs must had taken her, or worse, destroyed her.

Toots whimpered, "Those things are really smart. How are we going to beat them?"

"Well I'm not sure, dear," Mr. McGhee grumbled. "I think we need to stick to my original plan. Just go at them head-on. We will make a diversion and just run into the barn and get the Snow Globe."

Mr. McGhee drove the truck as Dante, Pistachio, and Lucky protected it from stragglers. The rest of the cherubs reorganized at Skeeter's house.

15

IT ALL LOOKS SO HOPELESS

Mr. McGhee pulled the truck into Skeeter's driveway, stopped, and looked over the situation. Rusty and Skeeter jumped from the bed and got into the cab with Mr. McGhee and Toots.

Mr. McGhee plotted, "This is what we need to do kids. Now listen closely. I am going to drive my truck up and get as close to the barn as we can. I'll create a diversion and we will run into the barn get the Snow Globe. Read it, and this will be over. It's that simple."

Mr. McGhee got out of his truck and requested, "Dante, you need to fly over to the barn door and break the cherubs' defenses. Create a path so that Pistachio can fly up behind you and open up the door, allowing access for the rest of us to get in." Pistachio and Dante listened to the plan and nodded agreeably.

"Everybody know the plan?" inquired Mr. McGhee.

Everyone motioned yes.

Mr. McGhee drove his truck, spun the tires, and blew the horn. He made as much noise as possible. Dante flew at the swarm of cherubs. He fought and swung with the precision of a championship boxer. Each punch he landed either busted a cherub or at least knocked one back. Mr. McGhee slid the truck sideways in front of the barn. The kids leapt out of the passenger side. Mr. McGhee hopped out the driver's side door and fired shotgun blasts to disperse the cherubs enough so that the kids could run into the barn. Pistachio was already there. He had the door open. Mr. McGhee threw his last grenade and the explosion scared everyone, especially the cherubs. It seemed they didn't like loud noises.

Rusty was the first one out of the truck. He ran as fast as he could. He made it through the door. The second one out was Toots. She also made it into the barn. Skeeter jumped out of the truck last and ran. A couple of the cherubs flew down and tripped Skeeter. He fell and lay on the ground, unprotected.

Mr. McGhee saw this, tried to run and save him, but he fell also. He was slow to pick himself back up. He aimed the shotgun at the cherubs above Skeeter and hoped to at least scare them away with the noise, but the gun went *click* when he fired. He was out of bullets. A few cherubs came at him; he swung the gun like a baseball bat and struck them down. He looked over and saw the cherubs had Skeeter surrounded and pinned him down.

Mr. McGhee headed back to the truck for his duffle bag to get ammunition, but the fall and all the physical exertion during the day had taken its toll on him. He ran with a limp as if he had pulled a muscle or broke a bone and he was out of breath. His age showed. It was painful for him to reach over the side of the truck bed, but he managed to grab his duffel bag, rummaged through it, and found only a few shells left. He loaded his gun.

The cherubs had lifted Skeeter off the ground and carried him away. Mr. McGhee quickly fired shots off, but did not want to hit Skeeter. His shots were merely a deterrent. They were out of reach. There was no way he could stop them. He saw Skeeter squirm as they carried him away.

Mr. McGhee thought, *I can't save him this way, we need the Snow Globe.* He fired off a couple more shots, cleared his path, and hobbled from the truck to get in the barn with the kids.

Toots and Rusty looked out of the door window and they saw what was happening to Skeeter.

Pistachio guarded the door. He bashed and clobbered any cherub that wanted to come into the barn. The kids noticed that Dante tried to make his way to the swarm that had Skeeter, but he was stopped by a wall of cherubs and some were armed with hammers, tools, sticks, and rocks.

Toots wailed, "We need to get Skeeter! What are they going to do with him?"

The kids watched what was going on. Mr. McGhee was now in the barn and shouted, "The Snow Globe! Read the Snow Globe!"

Rusty had it in his hand and held it up. He looked at it and blurted out, "*Permito sleepo!*"

That was nowhere close to what he needed to say, but it was the best form of Latin that Rusty could manage to come up with.

Rusty tried to read it multiple times to no avail. He could not do it. It was not working.

Mr. McGhee groaned, "It's not good out there," as he looked out at Dante.

Mr. McGee and the kids gazed out of the barn door. They saw Dante fighting valiantly. He had his hands full. With every swing he took, he knocked a few of the cherubs out of the fight. There were so many cherubs that swarmed around Dante that it was hard to even see him. The fight hovered in the air all around the barn. At one point the kids needed to move over to the side window to witness the action. It looked as if Dante held his own and that the swarm of cherubs had thinned just a little.

Then all of a sudden one of the cherubs acted like a kamikaze and flew right toward Dante. It curled up in a ball, smashed into him and broke his wing. This caused Dante to fly erratically. He crashed into the ground along with the mass of cherubs on him. Dante was able to get to his feet and he continued to fight. He threw punches left and right. He gave them everything he had and pushed them back. The scuffle moved around Skeeter's yard. Dante tried to get off the ground, but every time he did, he was knocked off-balance and back down. He kept getting up after each time he was knocked down. The fight took its toll on him. The cherubs had his wings almost completely destroyed and there was no hope for him ever to fly again. He continued a strong fight but started to weaken.

The mass of cherubs grabbed Dante's arms and pulled him back and exposed his chest. He struggled, but they overpowered him. The group of cherubs separated into two. One group held Dante down, and the other picked up an old fence post that Skeeter's dad had lying around. Ten or so cherubs grasped the post like a battering ram, and took flight.

With a twenty-yard running start, the cherubs flew with the post like a dive-bomber and headed toward Dante. They slammed it directly into his chest, knocked him to the ground and broke off a big piece of his shoulder and arm. They continued their relentless pursuit of him. They bashed, banged, hit, and swung until the swarm dispersed. They left a pile of rubble where the gang last saw Dante. This vicious attack had left him nothing more than a pile of gravel.

Disbelief and sadness had set in on our crew. The plan was falling apart. Skeeter was carried further and further away. Dante was destroyed and the Snow Globe did not work.

"This is hopeless," said Rusty.

Pistachio fought outside the door to keep the cherubs from getting in. Pistachio was created from marble and was a little stronger than the concrete cherubs. He was able to take more blows than they could dish out. Pistachio also had an aluminum baseball bat that he picked up from the bed of Mr. McGhee's truck. This definitely aided his defense immensely.

Toots was in tears. "They're carrying Skeeter away!" she screamed as she grabbed the Snow Globe. She held it up in the air and read it. She cried, sobbed and read the words, but it did not work for her either.

She looked through the Snow Globe and her eyes focused on the back wall of the barn. She noticed a few shelves on the wall that had a tarp on them. Something stuck out from one of the corners. It was a gargoyle's head. She ran over to the tarp and yanked it off, and to everyone's surprise, there were a bunch of gargoyles that Skeeter's mom made prior to the cherubs. No one bought them because they were not very good. The mold she used was not good quality and the casting process was poor. They appeared to be ugly, nasty, foul, hideous creatures, but for our crew they were the most beautiful things they had ever seen.

Toots exclaimed, "Lucky, use your magic. Bring these gargoyles to life. We need them to save Skeeter!"

Lucky flew into action and animated the fifteen gargoyles. Their features were not perfect. Their castings were crude, but they were gargoyles nonetheless. They were protectors. Guardians.

The gargoyles animated as Lucky touched them. One by one they woke up, crashed through the door that protected the gang, and helped Pistachio with the fight.

Mr. McGhee commented, "I believe the Snow Globe is not working for us because we did not read the saying when the creatures were first brought to life. I'm sure Skeeter needs to be the one to say the magic spell. The cherubs know this; that is why they have him. When they couldn't find it, they knew they had only two things they could do to stop us. Destroy the Snow Globe or destroy the person who said the incantation. That's why they have Skeeter."

The new regiment of gargoyles seemed overwhelmed, but held back the cherub army anyway. They were outnumbered, but they made a difference. The cherub army started to weaken.

Rusty, Toots, and Mr. McGhee were now able to chase after Skeeter. They saw where the cherubs had taken him. It was to a large pond, which in happier days was full of pleasure for the boys. They swam, fished, and boated there, but not today. The cherubs had Skeeter and dropped him in the water. The three watched helplessly from along the pond bank. It was as if in slow motion for them. They could see Skeeter as he struggled in the water. The cherubs dive-bombed him, hit him, picked him up and dunked him back down again and again.

Skeeter was around three hundred feet out in the middle of the pond. They looked around and a lot of the new gargoyles had been destroyed. Mr. McGhee jumped into the water and swam after Skeeter.

Rusty looked off to the east and he saw a sign of hope. Out of nowhere came flying the Paxton gargoyles. The four that Lucky brought to life at the museum. They made short work of the few cherubs that were there in Paxton City, destroyed them easily, and were here to help.

16

NOT MY TIME

"Nooooo! Nooooo! Stop! Stooooooop! Please don't!" screamed Skeeter as he hung suspended over the pond.

He dropped about twenty feet into the water and made a big splash. He popped his head out. He felt okay; nothing hurt, nothing seemed to be broken. He survived the fall into the water. He was okay and swam toward shore.

He heard a couple more splashes, and the cherubs entered with him. He felt them as they swam around. They tugged at his feet and clothes. The pressure on his legs pulled him under the water. He tried to fight. He kicked, squirmed and made an effort to free himself. He needed to get away from them. They held him under, and the more he struggled the weaker he became.

Skeeter held his breath and tried to get free but he couldn't. The last attempt he made to get to the surface almost got him there. He flailed his arms and tried to grab for something that was not there. This allowed him to break free from the cherubs that held him under, and gave him a chance to get to the surface. He took in a good full gulp of air and then was pulled under again. His mind raced, but every-thing around him moved in slow motion.

He thought to himself, *How can this be happening?* He had just begun to live. There was so much for him to do with his life. This couldn't be the end. He could not give up. He needed to fight these nasty little creatures with every breath in his body. They couldn't hold him down. They couldn't stop him. He wanted to fall in love. He wanted to get mar-ried. He wanted to raise his own children, and grow old with Alexandria. This could not be the end. He would never let these monsters take away his dreams. There was no fear in his heart. He was not scared.

The cherubs continued to pull Skeeter under. He needed to breathe again. He could feel the oxygen leave his body. He had that feeling you get when you hold your breath as long as you could. The feeling of suffocation and anxiety. Panic and fear did not just set in, but it consumed his every thought. He had used up all the oxygen in his lungs and the lack of fear he had moments before changed quickly, and he was very scared. He couldn't breathe. He was underwater doing anything to stay alive.

He thought to himself, *Oh to get one more breath of air into his lungs. Just one more time.* That was when it happened. Skee-ter stopped struggling, and the cherubs let go and flew away.

17

THE HERO OF ROARING SPRINGS

Mr. McGhee made it to the middle of the pond. He saw Skeeter's lifeless body floating there. He grabbed Skeeter and pulled him toward land as fast as he could. Three of the Paxton gargoyles soared above and protected Mr. McGhee. They kept the remaining cherubs away from Skeeter and Mr. McGhee. The kids watched from the shore.

Toots was crying.

Rusty screamed, "Come on! Come on you can do it!" Mr. McGhee paddled, and kicked, with all his strength, all his might, all his determination. He neared the edge of the water. Pistachio flew over, gripped onto Skeeter's clothes, and helped Mr. McGhee to pull Skeeter further onto dry land.

Everyone gathered around Skeeter's lifeless thin frame. He lay there very pale. His clothes were ripped and torn. He was battered, scraped, and bruised.

Toots screamed, "Do something! Do something!"

Rusty was crying. Everyone was crying. Their friend was dead.

Toots was on her knees and cradled Skeeter's lifeless body. She went into shock and became silent. She didn't scream hysterically. She held him in total disbelief. The only emotion she showed was a single teardrop that ran down her cheek.

From out of nowhere they heard a very loud, ear-piercing scream. It was Lucky. This was the first sound that Lucky had made in many years. Somehow Lucky knew if Skeeter didn't catch him all those years back, he would have broken and not have been here today. Lucky's screams were cries of rage against his fellow cherubs for what they had done. Sadness had been pent up inside of Lucky, even before this had begun. He could not believe this happened to his buddy Skeeter, his best friend.

The wails that came out of Lucky seemed to last forever but it was only for a moment. Lucky flew over, grabbed what was left of Skeeter's shirt, pulled him from Toots's arms, and with all his might picked him up off the ground about a foot. He could not carry him far and dropped him. He pulled at Skeeter's shirt and dropped him again. His anger had gotten the best of him. Everyone continued to look in disbelief and could not stop Lucky. He continued to hop up and down on Skeeter's chest.

His misdirected anger and rage inadvertently pumped Skeeter's chest. He didn't realize what he had done, but Lucky gave Skeeter a form of CPR that used only chest compressions instead of mouth-to-mouth resuscitation.

Oxygen moved in and out of Skeeter's small and lifeless body and then, out of nowhere Skeeter began to cough the water out of his lungs. He took a big gasp of air and started to breathe again.

Their friend was alive.

A sigh of relief and the sounds of joy, happiness, and laughter started to grow among this little crew. Skeeter was okay. He felt abused, sore and as if he were hit by a train, but was conscious and aware of his surroundings.

Everyone near Skeeter could hear that sound of children's laughter as it grew.

There were nowhere near as many as there were before. The Paxton gargoyles and Pistachio made sure of that. Yet the cherub army began to form off in the distance, and planned another assault. Pistachio and three of the remaining Paxton gargoyles stood guard; one was destroyed in the last battle. They all watched every move the swarming cherubs made.

Rusty reached into his pocket, pulled out the orb and said, "It's up to you buddy. This ain't working for us."

Skeeter was still dazed. He got to his feet, regained his balance, grabbed the Snow Globe from Rusty, looked at the words, extended his arm out fully, reached to the sky, opened his hand, and allowed the Snow Globe to rest in his open palm. He proceeded to say aloud, in an extraordinarily loud voice, *"Sit eos somno!"* Let them sleep.

The orb started to levitate from Skeeter's hand as it did before. Rusty and Skeeter turned their backs and crouched down. They knew what was going to happen. Then a crack of lightning shot from the orb to the sky and made a terrible clap of thunder. It sent the kids backwards. Clouds formed rapidly and the red rain began again. This time it fell from the sky.

The kids noticed Pistachio first. His green smooth complexion started to stain with the red tint. He slowly landed and returned back into his original form; a kind of lucidity came across him and he lost all life. Next, they saw the Paxton gargoyles land and the same thing happened to them; their movement slowly came to a stop and they too went back to sleep.

The gang looked over at the cherubs. They panicked and scattered in every direction. They couldn't escape the red rain and one by one they all dropped out of the sky, splashed down in the water, hit the ground, and ceased to exist. The red rain continued for a few minutes. Everyone was a mess, covered in blood-colored stains, but they laughed, and were happy and joyous.

The red rain slowly changed to water and washed away any evidence of what happened on that day. The world, or at least their little portion of the world, seemed to be back to normal, with the exception of broken windows and statues.

Skeeter was okay, and everyone was happy.

The kids talked amongst themselves and rejoiced. Everyone was hugging Skeeter, when he noticed something and inquired, "Where is Mr. McGhee?"

Rusty asserted, "He is down by the pond. He pulled you out. He saved your life."

Everyone turned at the same time, looked toward the pond and in the excitement, they had failed to notice that Mr. McGhee had collapsed. The swim out to save Skeeter and the excitement of the day had taken its toll on him. They all ran to where Mr. McGhee was and huddled around him. His breathing was very short, and he was not able to take a full breath. Skeeter dropped down on his knees alongside Mr. McGhee and moved close to him, near his chest. He could hear Mr. McGhee try to say something. Skeeter put his ear next to his mouth.

Mr. McGhee, in a very faint and weakened voice whispered, "Get those no-good dirty vermin," and he closed his eyes for the last time.

"We did, we got 'em," sobbed Skeeter as he tried to hold back tears, but it was too much for this little man to handle and he broke down. Mr. McGhee's heart gave out while saving Skeeter, and he passed away. Skeeter lay his weight down on Mr. McGhee's chest and put his arms around him, and cried. "Why, why, why?! We were so mean to him. He didn't do anything to us. We just went along with the people in town. We were wrong. We were the trespassers. We were the brats."

Toots was sorrowful also. She knelt next to Skeeter and consoled him the best she could. She put her arm around him and whispered in his ear, "He protected us and that was the kind of man he was. We never could have done this without him. He was a hero."

Skeeter got to his feet and they both looked at Rusty. They saw that his eyes teared up. Rusty didn't know what to do. He was the tough guy in the group but he couldn't hide his feelings anymore either. He had made a special bond with Mr. McGhee too and it hit him hard.

The three kids moved in close and put their arms around each other.

"I know Mr. McGhee made us swear that we wouldn't tell the truth about what happened here," said Skeeter, "but that's not right."

"I know exactly what you are thinking," commented Toots.

"Thinking about what?" asked Rusty.

"I think we should make a new vow," insisted Skeeter. "I say together we let everyone know the truth about what happened here, and how Mr. McGhee didn't just rescue us, but he saved the whole town."

Skeeter put his hand out, palm down, then Toots placed hers on top of his, and finally Rusty.

"I swear," all three said together, and with that the kids made a pact that no lie ever told could outshine the truth of what kind of man Mr. McGhee truly was.

18

DEBT REPAID

The sun awakened a new day. The town of Roaring Springs and everyone affected started to clean up the mess of yesterday's tragedy.

Skeeter came down the stairs, gave his mom a hug and started crying, "Momma, I can't believe that. I never got a chance to thank him for pulling me from the pond. I was sure that I had more time to get to know him and make up for all times I disrespected him. I wish we didn't treat him the way we did. He was a good man. Look at what he did. He could've stayed at his home and just protected his house. All we ever did was mock him and laugh at him. He was willing to stand up for us, fight with us, fight for us. I can never say I'm sorry. He saved my life twice. What am I going to do?" Skeeter rested his head in his mom's shoulder.

"Skeeter, I know Mr. McGhee forgave you for everything, or he would not have helped you," assured Skeeter's mom in a comforting voice. "I know you miss him, and can never repay him personally for what he has done. The best way you can honor him, is be the best person you can be. The man that you are and the man that you will become are defined by your words and your actions. Learn from his sacrifice and grow up to be a strong, caring young man. Always do the next right thing and know that someday you will meet him again, and you'll be able to thank him then."

Skeeter felt sorrowful and walked away from his mom. He headed outside, carrying a heavy weight on his shoulders. He opened the kitchen door, stood on the porch, and looked at the mess that used to be his yard. He tried to decide where he would start cleaning up and just then he heard that ominous child's laughter again. It made his blood curdle and he cringed.

He thought to himself, *Oh no, not this again!* He looked up toward the laughter and saw Lucky flying in the open rafters of the porch, in the exact place where he first met him. Somehow, he knew what was going to happen. He had done this before. He was a lot older and different than the other cherubs that Skeeter's mom made. Lucky took shelter on the porch, up in the collar ties before the red rain fell, and this protected him.

Lucky flew down and grabbed at Skeeter. He pulled on his shirt, motioned for Skeeter to follow, flew away a little bit and pointed.

"What is it Lucky, what do you want?" inquired Skeeter. "Do you want me to follow you?"

Lucky shook his head yes and flew down the driveway. Skeeter hopped on his bicycle and followed. Lucky led the way. He started, then stopped and waited for Skeeter. He flew a little further and did this multiple times so Skeeter could keep up. Lucky was excited and traveled the same route that Rusty and Skeeter used to go to the firework battle area. They went down the path that led to Mr. McGhee's house. They came to the barbed wire fence. Skeeter remembered all the time he snuck through there, but this time was different. This time he wasn't scared of being caught. He just had a sense of emptiness and regret. They passed through the wire and rode across the well-groomed yard. Skeeter stopped and took the time to actually admire what the yard looked like. He was amazed at how beautiful it was. He knew now why Mr. McGhee was so mad when they went through. It was his own little memorial, a shrine to his wife, and he didn't like it being disrespected.

Lucky continued to lead Skeeter. He brought him back past the burned down Fortress, over the busted-up bridge, and into the area behind the old farmhouse. The area looked different though. All the brush that Rusty and Skeeter used to cover up the old root cellar, "the Cave," had been pulled away, exposing the entrance. Skeeter made his way through the piles of brush and looked in the opening of the root cellar.

He poked his head in and to his amazement, he saw a glorious sight. The sun shined in and illuminated a vast treasure trove of loot. It looked so beautiful, how the diamonds reflected light on the golden objects. It was almost too bright to gaze at. Lucky had led Skeeter to the stash of all the shiny little things that the cherubs had taken from town: jewelry, rare coins, gold, diamonds, and so much more.

The immense riches that were there probably added up to millions of dollars, but there was one thing that Skeeter noticed most. He went over to the pile and grabbed a home-made wooden case. He blew the dust off and read a hand-carved inscription: "Mildred McGhee's Silver Spoons." It was Mr. McGhee's wife's spoon collection, the one she cherished so much. It represented the goals and accomplishments she had done in her life by documenting the places she had traveled. It was her own personal time vault.

Skeeter knew what he was going to do. He stepped out of the Cave and covered up the entrance the best he could so no one would discover the stash. He didn't want anyone bad to steal everything before he had the chance to return it.

He went back to Mr. McGhee's house and walked up to the opened door carrying the spoon case. The place was in shambles. He was not sure if he could continue to go inside the house because of what happened to him there yesterday, but he mustered up the courage to walk in. He looked around for a bit. He cautiously moved from room to room, expecting to see a cherub around every corner. That would have been okay if he did because Lucky was there to protect him, but none were there.

He finally saw the mark on the wall where the case had hung. You could tell from its position it was extremely important to Mrs. McGhee. It was the focal point for that particular wall and all the other pictures were positioned in a way that complemented the spoon case. The mark was actually a stain on the paint and it told a story. One could tell how the stain changed over the years. The case was small at one point, and was not able to hold enough spoons. Mr. McGhee always needed to build a bigger one. This happened multiple times throughout the couple's life and the mark revealed that.

Skeeter stood in the same spot as Mr. McGhee did all those times, when he changed the case out for a new one. He placed Mrs. McGhee's spoons back on the wall. He lined up the nails with the holes in the back of the case.

Something strange and wonderful happened to him at that moment. He felt a push from behind, like someone bumped into him and a flash ran through his head. In an instant, he saw the life of a boy playing, riding an antique bike and shooting a slingshot. The boy grew up to be a young man. He saw that the man was a soldier and in a battle of some sort. His intuition told him who it was but he couldn't be exactly sure, though. The images he witnessed were a first-person perspective and they continued. The man met a girl, grew older, got married, worked on a farm, and the last thing to pass through his mind was the final time the spoon case was placed on the wall.

Skeeter connected to Mr. McGhee's consciousness, in a spiritual way, while being in the exact same spot as he stood through some of the proudest moments of his life. Skeeter was able to see in a flash all the important things that had happened to Mr. McGhee in his lifetime. It ran through his mind in and instant but he remembered everything. It was as if Mr. McGhee was in the room and told the story of his life to Skeeter through his own eyes. He left nothing out. The orb must have changed Skeeter in some way. It did not freak him out but just the opposite; he felt it was a blessing. He had the chance to see what kind of man Mr. McGhee really was, and not the lies that the townspeople told about him.

Skeeter rode home as rapidly as he could. He arrived at his house and saw Lucky sat in the same spot he did for years. Lucky was a statue again. Skeeter passed by and looked at him.

Skeeter sighed, "Oh man! What happened, Lucky? Why are you not moving? You were just okay."

Skeeter was bummed because he lost his friend and at that moment Lucky winked at Skeeter. Lucky was hiding in plain sight. Skeeter made the "yes" sign with his fist and gave a thumbs-up to show Lucky that he knew what he was up to.

Skeeter ran into the house and yelled, "Mom, guess what I found. I found all the—"

Skeeter's mom interrupted him with the "shut up open hand" gesture, not allowing him to finish. She was watching the TV news from a neighboring town.

"This just in. The streets of Maiden Creek Township are being overrun by hundreds of yard gnomes. Yes, you heard that right folks. The township has been overrun by those cute little bearded yard decorations. Somehow, they have come to life and are damaging property, wreaking havoc everywhere and detaining citizens. The authorities are suggesting that you stay in your homes and wait for further instruction..." reported the local news broadcaster.

"No way!" declared Skeeter, "Mom, we gotta do something!"

Skeeter ran out of the house and announced, "Come on Lucky...we have a lot more work to do!"

Acknowledgements

A special thank goes to:

The love of my life Maureen Stangle for giving me the encouragement and confidence to take on this project and always being there for me. This accomplishment is as much mine as it is yours. I love you Baby.

Tom Breiner for putting me in the right directions early on with this story and everything else, in life, you did for me.

Rose Jamieson, Claire Rohloff, Annie and Mark Loos for having an interest in my idea and helping me correct my mistakes.

Rita Marie Stangle Miller and Rev. James G. Tucker for helping me get the Latin translations right.

Robert "B. J." Lilly for being a lifelong friend.

Steve Porter for helping me make this dream come true.

Without all of you, none of this would have been possible. Thank you.

About the Author

Francis "Frankie" Stangle comes from a large family, and being a story teller to his over 30 nephews and nieces, has finally decided to put his words down in print to share them with the world. He writes his books from the same house he was born in. He spent his youth playing in the neighborhood stream, biking and having fun with his friends. He eats way too much chocolate, but don't tell his wife, and he loves to stare up at the night sky with her. He lets his mind wander about the universe and the secrets that the stars, nebulas, and distant galaxies hold. When he grows up, he wants to be an astronaut.

Some strange coincidences have happened to him in his life, and many have found their way into this book. He knows that someone has been looking over him, protecting him in some way and someday he will be able to thank them.

Frank believes that every child needs to grab ahold of a dream and hold onto it until they make it come true, and that every adult has the responsibility to make sure that happens.

Shiny Little Things is his debut novel.

Follow on:
FACEBOOK   Frank Stangle
FACEBOOK GROUP   Shiny Little Things – A Novel
INSTAGRAM   frankstangle
TWITTER   @FrankStangle
WEBSITE   www.frankstangle.com
EMAIL   frank@frankstangle.com

Made in the USA
Middletown, DE
09 June 2022

66883716R00076